THE EMPEROR'S SEAL

THE EMPEROR'S SEAL

TOUCHING TIME BOOK 1

AMANDA ROBERTS

Red Empress Publishing
www.RedEmpressPublishing.com

Copyright © Amanda Roberts
www.AmandaRobertsWrites.com

Cover by Cherith Vaughan
https://www.facebook.com/coversbycherith

ALSO BY AMANDA ROBERTS

Fiction

Threads of Silk

The Man in the Dragon Mask

The Qing Dynasty Mysteries

Murder in the Forbidden City

Murder in the British Quarter

Murder at the Peking Opera

The Touching Time Series

The Child's Curse

The Emperor's Seal

The Empress's Dagger

The Slave's Necklace

The Empress in Disguise Trilogy

Empress in Disguise

Empress in Hiding

Empress in Danger

Nonfiction

The Crazy Dumplings Cookbook

Crazy Dumplings II: Even Dumplinger

ONE

"*D*o it," the empress commanded.

Carefully, as if it contained a snake that could bite her, Jiayi pulled up the long sleeves of her robe and took the box in her hands. She inhaled slow deep breaths as she closed her eyes. She never knew what to expect, so she had to be prepared for anything.

When she opened her eyes again, she was surrounded by running horses. People screamed as they ran for cover. The men riding the horses brandished weapons, and they slashed and hacked at the people around them. Jiayi turned left and right, searching for a way out before she too was trampled. She had never died during one of her visions before, but she didn't know what would happen to her in real life if she did. She didn't want to take the chance. One of the riders stopped to skewer a man not far from her. The victim screamed as blood shot from his body like a fountain. Jiayi was terrified, but there was nothing she could do for him. She had to take care of herself. The stopped horse caused a break in the sea of galloping beasts. Jiayi had to run while she had the chance. She had no idea where she was going, why the box the empress handed her sent her to this place, this time, but she had to find it—the emperor's seal. Somehow this body, this woman she was inhabiting, had a connection to it. She had to trust that this woman would lead her to the answer.

She ran as far as she could, away from the battle. Up on a hill, she saw a large tent and many men on horseback watching the fray below. Why they were only watching, she did not know. She looked down at her clothing and saw she was dressed in the garb of a Manchu noblewoman. The men who were watching were also dressed as Manchu. At least she wasn't running toward the enemy. She scurried up the hill as quickly as she could.

"Please! Help me!" she screamed when they were within earshot.

The men looked down at her in utter surprise, as if they only just now saw her. It was possible. Jiayi had no idea what her manifestations in the visions looked like to other people.

"Lady Caigiya!" one of the men dressed as a general called out. He pointed to her and two of his men ran down to her side and helped her up. "What happened? How did you get down there?" the general asked when she finally made it to him.

"I...I don't know," she mumbled. "I must have been lost..."

The answer seemed to satisfy the general. He nodded again to his men. "Take her to the emperor. He must be worried about her."

Jiayi doubted that very much. She had never known an emperor to worry over a woman, but she allowed herself to be led along. She was taken to a large tent, one big and grand enough to be an imperial residence at the Forbidden

City. When the heavy curtains were drawn back, it was so dark inside she could see nothing. She was ungraciously ushered inside and the curtains were dropped closed behind her. The room was shockingly quiet. She could hear low voices of men talking but could hardly hear the sounds of the battle raging just below so thick were the walls of the tent. After a moment, her eyes began to adjust to the low light of the braziers scattered throughout the room.

On the far side was a large table, and several men stood around it in a heated discussion. Around the tent, along the walls, were fashionably dressed ladies and many children. If the emperor was here, these had to be his ladies—his wives and concubines—and his children, the princes and princesses. Why were they here, in the midst of a dangerous battle? Not for the first time Jiayi wished she knew something of history. Even names and dates would help her understand her visions so much more.

She took a few steps closer to the men in the middle of the room. The general had said she should be taken to the emperor, but did he just mean here, in this room, or to his side?

One of the men looked up at her and his face brightened. "Cai!" he called out as he ran to her. "My beloved," he cooed as he held her hand. "What happened to you?" he asked.

Cai! Of course. Caigiya was her full name, but she was more commonly known as Lady Cai, the most loved—and the most scandalous—of Emperor Daoguang's women. Jiayi did not need a formal history lesson to know who she was now. Any woman who lived in the palace would know of the infamous Lady Cai, the one who stole an emperor's heart.

But there was no time for her to recite the legend of

their love now. She needed to find the seal. If she failed again, the empress would be highly displeased...and no one wanted to be in the empress's bad graces.

"I...I was lost. Horses were running and men were screaming..." she said, her voice cracking.

"I am so sorry you got caught up in that. The rebels, they came upon us so swiftly. I was a fool to try to take my family to Jehol during such a time..." the emperor lamented as he wrapped a comforting arm around her.

Jiayi was putting a few pieces together. The emperor and his family must have been traveling from Peking to the Mountain Palace north of Peking in Jehol when they were sat upon by a rebel army. What rebels, she had no idea, but it did not seem important right now.

"I am fine," Jiayi said as she tried to smile. "I am here with you now."

The emperor smiled back and kissed her tenderly. She nearly pulled away. Such moments always shocked her. She had never been kissed in real life. She was an innocent maiden who had spent most of her life sequestered in the empress's palace. But this was not the first time a man in one of her visions kissed her. Some had done more...She had learned to suppress her real feelings and let the body of her host take over. She needed to remain calm and pretend everything was normal. She needed the emperor to lead her to the seal. It had to be here.

The emperor stepped back and smiled at her. "You are sure everything is fine?" he asked.

She nodded. "Of course. I was only worried for you. Is there any way I can help you?" she asked.

He reached up and playfully touched her nose. "It is as if you can read my thoughts," he said. "Follow me."

She did as she was told. The emperor took her hand and

led her to the table surrounded by the other men. They looked anything but happy to have her in their presence, scowling and crossing their arms. They were not used to discussing important matters in the presence of a woman. Jiayi could not help but smile to herself at that. In her time, several decades later, China was ruled by a woman.

"Your Majesty," one of the men said. "Surely there is another way—"

"We must protect the seal," the emperor said firmly. "The seal represents the emperor—myself and every emperor who had come before me and who will come after until the end of time—and the Mandate of Heaven. We are under attack here! If the barbarians get their hands on it, they could use it to overthrow the dynasty! If I die today, they could find the seal and use it to claim the empire for themselves. It must be hidden, just for now."

"But to trust a woman?" another of the ministers piped up.

The emperor laughed. "Women are the best at hiding things! Every chance they get they will spirit away a bit of money or a jewel or even a piece of fine clothing and you will never see it again. Why do you think you must always buy them new things?"

The other men joined in the laughter, but Jiayi blushed. It was partly true. Most women could not earn their own money, so they had to hide small amounts away for an emergency. A woman never knew when she might lose the favor of her husband or mother-in-law or other benefactor and have nowhere to go and no food to eat. Even in the service of the empress, Jiayi feared the day she would no longer be useful to her and find herself back on the street.

The emperor snapped his fingers. A eunuch ran up and placed a large box on the table. It was the same box that

Jiayi was holding in her real hands—the box that contained the seal. The box was red lacquered with golden dragons painted on it. It was much larger than it needed to be, but the box's interior had many layers of protective red silk to cushion the seal.

The emperor opened the box and reverently lifted the seal. The seal had been forged from pure gold hundreds of years ago. The base of the seal was square, but on the top was an ornately carved dragon—the symbol of the emperor. The dragon's eyes were set with rubies that glistened in the firelight from the braziers. Each of the four sides of the seal had cloisonné images that were blue in the background with two dragons—eight in all—reaching for a flaming pearl. The pearl symbolized wisdom, prosperity, power, and immortality—all qualities the emperor possessed.

The beauty of the seal and the weight of its meaning took Jiayi's breath away. She was so close. Her hands started to tremble and sweat beaded on her forehead. The whole room started to blur. As the emperor turned to her, it was as though the world had slowed down. Jiayi realized what was happening—she was waking up! She was losing her grip on the vision and would soon be back in the presence of the empress. She had to find out what happened to the seal before it was too late.

The emperor stepped toward her so slowly it was as if he was moving through thick mud. Jiayi tried to walk to him but was nearly frozen in place. "My love," she called out, willing him to hurry without causing suspicion.

"My dear Lady Cai," he said as he held out the seal. "I need you to hide this for me. Do you promise to keep it safe and reveal it to no one but me when it is once again safe to do so?" It sounded as though he was calling to her through water.

"Yes, yes, my love. Of course," she said. The world blurred further. She could no longer see the table, the braziers, or the angry faces of the men nearby.

"Into your hands, I entrust all of China."

She tried to hold out her hands, but she could not move quickly enough. The emperor released the seal and it slipped through her fingers, crashing to the ground.

"*Jiayi...*" she thought she heard the emperor say, but his voice sounded far away even though he was right in front of her.

"What?" she asked.

"*Jiayi...*" His voice was little more than a whisper as the world went black.

As Jiayi woke, she heard her name being called louder and louder.

"Jiayi! Jiayi, answer me! Did you find it? Do you know where the seal is?"

Jiayi opened her eyes and the empress was right in front of her. She started as the hard eyes looked deep into her own.

"Jiayi! Answer me! What did you see?"

"Lady Cai..." Jiayi said as she tried to recall the details of the vision. "The emperor gave the seal to Lady Cai."

She heard other women in the room gasp. She looked around and saw the empress's other ladies, her attendants and maids, all looking at her. While the empress kept Jiayi's powers secret from her ministers and male counselors, she did not bother hiding Jiayi from her friends and ladies— her real advisors.

"You mean *the* Lady Cai? The one the emperor nearly gave up the throne for?" one of the ladies, Princess Der Ling, asked. "He truly trusted her that much?"

Jiayi nodded. "He loved her," she said.

"But what about the seal?" the empress snapped, grabbing Jiayi's arm and shaking her.

She knew the empress would be angry when she found out Jiayi did not know where it was. But maybe she could give her enough information to temper her anger.

"There was a battle, on the road to Jehol. Some barbarians. I don't know who," she explained. "The emperor feared that they would kill him and steal the seal. He wanted Lady Cai to hide it, to protect it."

"*And?*" The empress was shaking. She held her hands out as if Jiayi was in possession of the seal and could simply hand it over to her.

"And...I...I dropped it," Jiayi said, tears forming in her eyes. "I'm sorry, but the vision ended before he could hand it to me. I don't know where it is. But he certainly gave it to Lady Cai! If we know where the battle took place, she must have hidden it nearby and..."

The empress slapped Jiayi so hard across the face she thought her neck snapped. She held her breath, afraid to make the slightest noise and possibly invite more of the empress's wrath. The room was utterly silent. None of the other women dared to go to Jiayi's aid. After a moment that seemed like much longer, the empress stumbled back. Jiayi finally sucked in a breath as everyone else in the room audibly exhaled. She straightened her neck, but kept her moist eyes downturned.

"So close...so close..." the empress muttered.

"We can try again," one of the other women suggested. She picked up the box and shoved it into Jiayi's hands, but nothing happened.

"You know it doesn't work that way," another of the other women angrily whispered, slapping her hands away.

"But Jiayi is right," Der Ling said. "If Lady Cai had the

box on the way to Jehol, that narrows the search considerably."

The empress sat down in her chair, looking as worn and exhausted as Jiayi felt. She was quiet for a moment, as if considering her options. Finally, she nodded her head. "Yes, it is time. Bring him to me..."

TWO

*S*ummoned by the empress! Zhihao could hardly believe he was about to be presented to the empress herself. Fine, the *dowager* empress, but no one called her that. Everyone knew that the emperor was only a ceremonial figure at best. The empress was the real power behind the throne.

This would not be the first time Zhihao had seen the empress. He had first met her many years ago, when he was but a boy of twelve. He had been an outstanding student and was selected as part of an elite group of boys to study in Britain, part of an initiative between the empress and her top counselor, Prince Gong, to become a more modern and international government. The empress financed the education of dozens of young men abroad in the hopes that they would come back and serve in top positions in the court and in Chinese society and help modernize the country.

It hadn't worked. The old men of the court were not willing to give up their positions so easily to this new crop of young modern thinkers when they returned. Most of the young men had to find secular positions when they arrived back home—which their families did not approve of. Zhihao had always been hardheaded, though, and he refused to let his education go to waste. With the help of Prince Gong, Zhihao had been given a teaching and research position at Peking University in the history department. The job was not glamorous or easy, but it was nearly as dirty as the hands-on digs he had been on in Egypt. There were no large-scale archeology projects in China, so he was mostly limited to reading and preserving ancient texts—dusty, crumbling old things—that were haphazardly shelved in the university library.

But the last time he had seen the empress, it was not a private audience. He did not speak to her and she did not address him directly. He had only been one among a group of boys at a formal presentation to the empress before they were sent abroad. He had heard nothing from her since that day. He thought she had forgotten he existed. What was one lowly academic to her? Suffice to say, the summons to appear before her and the highest ranking court magistrates was a shock, and an honor. What could she possibly want from him?

Even though he was far more comfortable in a British style suit and bowler hat, he thought it best to dress more conservatively for the empress. She had taken steps over the years to modernize the country, but he had heard she was quite old-fashioned. One would expect nothing less from a nearly seventy-year-old woman. He imagined she was much like Queen Victoria before her death—the monarch of a country barreling into the modern age but bound by tradition. He didn't shave the front of his head, though he did have a queue. Like all Chinese men, he had never cut his hair, but as a Han Chinese who had lived abroad, he could never bring himself to shave the front half of his head. He wore a conical silk hat with red fringe typical of scholars, but he added a hat pin that had been a gift and he always wore. He also wore round-framed spectacles. He spent far too much time squinting over ancient faded texts, which had already taken its toll on his vision.

He could not help but pace as he waited in the formal audience hall for the arrival of the empress. No one else, save a couple of eunuch servants, were in attendance. He was surprised since he was under the impression that this was to be a meeting with the empress and her advisors. He felt very alone and unnerved.

Finally, a gong was struck and a voice announced the arrival of the empress. Zhihao dropped to his knees and kowtowed before the thrones. The empress entered and climbed up on the raised dais. Her throne was only slightly to the side of the dragon throne—the emperor's throne— but it was set higher. The empress, even though she was the true ruler of China, would never dare sit on the dragon throne. Above the emperor's throne was a giant carved golden dragon holding a large pearl in its mouth. The carving and the dragon throne had been there since the creation of the Forbidden City during the Ming Dynasty. Legend said that if anyone but the emperor sat on the dragon throne, the dragon would release the pearl and the usurper would be crushed. The empress wanted it to be clear that *she* was the person in charge—thus her literally elevated position—but even she had enough healthy super-stition to not sit on the dragon throne.

Still, no men entered the room. The empress was only attended by her ladies and eunuchs.

"Zhihao, son of Dulong," the empress called out.

Zhihao sat up, but he kept his gaze low. "Your Majesty," he said. "You honor me with your presence."

The empress nodded. "I am pleased you have come. I am in need of your assistance."

"I would give my all in your service, Your Majesty," he said.

She nodded again. "You were not yet born when the foreigners destroyed my Summer Palace, were you?" she asked.

"No, your majesty," he said. "But my father was. He was there, in service to the Xianfeng Emperor. He saw the palace just before the catastrophe. He said it was the most splendid palace the world had ever known."

The empress sucked in a deep breath. "It was...it was. I have done my best to rebuild parts of it from my memory, but it is not the same. Hundreds of years of artisanship, thousands of buildings, millions of artifacts, trinkets, paintings...all snuffed out..."

Zhihao could tell that to this day the empress mourned the loss of her magnificent Summer Palace. It was well-known how much she loved it. She had spent the last thirty years trying to replace it, much to the chagrin of her over-taxed people.

"The British are politically our allies," she said. "But they can never truly be trusted. They have stolen countless items from us to sell in England or display in their own palaces."

Zhihao knew this was true. While he was studying in London, he loved visiting the British Museum and exploring the "Treasures of the Orient" exhibits. The items had all been stolen or taken from homes, shrines, and burial sites around China and India and other Asian countries, not given willingly. While he hated knowing how the museum procured its wares, it was one of his few connections to his homeland for many years. He could spend hours looking at a single carving or piece of embroidery, studying every intricate detail.

"I have had to make endless concessions to the foreign powers—the British, the Germans, the Americans, and now, even the Japanese—all in the name of *peace*." She very nearly spat the word peace as if it were acid on her tongue. "They have land, customs rights, ports, Christians running amok, their own cities, their own laws..." She shook her head. "The foreigners are a people apart in our own country. They can do whatever they want and we have to accept it. You know this."

Zhihao sighed. It was true. Foreigners had even murdered Chinese citizens but could not be prosecuted for their crimes under Chinese law. They were supposed to be punished under the laws of their own countries, but that never happened.

"This is true, Your Majesty," he finally said. "I appreciate my education abroad, but I cannot condone the way the foreigners freely ignore our laws and run roughshod over our own people."

The empress nodded, seemingly happy with his answer. She clearly wanted to make sure that he was on her side. That he was genuinely Chinese and had not been corrupted by the "foreign devils" before she explained the reason she had summoned him.

"I am old," the empress said. "I will not live forever. While I hope to live for many more years, I know I need to plan for my country's future. I need to make way for my nephew and his heirs to rule after I am gone. And I need to preserve my country's heritage for all the generations of Chinese to come.

"I have heard that several of the foreign governments have been sending historians and archeologists into China to learn about our history and search for lost artifacts. If they wanted to do this with our cooperation, I would be glad of it, but I believe they are simply stealing our heritage! I am hearing reports of family tombs that have been completely looted. Ancient shrines and temples are being taken apart brick by brick. Our own history is being leeched away from us every day. Have you heard of this?" she asked.

"There have been rumors, Your Majesty," Zhihao said. "I have heard that the British customs official has been looking the other way when ships laden with cultural items leave our ports. I have spoken with my colleagues at the university about it and have suggested that we need to start locating and cataloging historical items ourselves so we can have an accurate record. The foreigners will not be able to steal from us so easily if we have better records—"

"Yes, yes," the empress interrupted and nodded. "I have heard of your interest in preserving our heritage. That is why I sent for you. I need you to find something for me."

"Of course, Your Majesty," he said. "Anything."

"I need you to find the emperor's seal."

Zhihao's jaw dropped. He could not hide the shock on his face and blushed when he heard some of the ladies giggle. He must have looked ridiculous.

"The...the emperor's s-s-seal?" he stammered. The emperor's seal was the single most important item the emperor owned. It was the physical embodiment of the Mandate of Heaven—his godly ordained right to rule. More than that, it was a practical item. It was used to stamp imperial edits, to make laws and pronouncements valid. If the seal was missing, what had the emperor and empress been using to stamp the edicts?

"Don't...don't you have it, Your Majesty?" he finally asked.

"The seal went missing long ago. During the reign of the Daoguang Emperor."

"It has been missing for more than fifty years?" Zhihao asked in disbelief. He held his hand to his mouth. Zhihao liked to think of himself as a reasonable man, one led by reason and logic, not superstition. But if the emperor's seal had been lost so long ago, that might explain China's descent. Since the first Opium War in the 1830s, China had been plagued by wars, rebellions, droughts, poverty. Many people blamed the empress since it was unnatural for a woman to be on the throne. But if the seal was lost, so was the Mandate of Heaven. The Celestial Beings no longer shined on the Middle Kingdom and the people were merely floundering. The Manchu had no right to the throne! Zhihao could feel his anger rising. The whole monarchy was a sham!

"I have been using a copy of the seal, one given to me as a gift by my late husband, the Xianfeng Emperor," the empress said, interrupting his thoughts. "I need you to find the seal. The *real* seal. There are those who do not think that we Manchu should rule China anymore."

Zhihao had to not breathe to keep from snorting. That was certainly an understatement. There had been rumblings of overthrowing the Qing Dynasty for decades, but the rumblings had become a dull roar as of late. In the past, no one had given an alternative. Trade one emperor for another? That could be worse than the current system. But there were new rules of thought developing—constitutional monarchies, socialism, communism, democracy. The talk was no longer about *if* the imperial family would be overthrown, but *when*, and what system would take its place. Zhihao was in favor of ousting the Qing, but he had never said such out loud. He was a thinker and listener, not a revolutionary. But when the fight came, he knew what side he would be on.

"The sudden reappearance of the real seal will give the emperor, my dear nephew, the blessing of the people. His rule will be assured. It will at least keep the foreigners from finding it. Can you imagine what would happen if the British or the Russians got their hands on the seal?"

Zhihao had to admit, foreigners finding the seal would be infinitely worse than the empress getting it back. If nothing else, the seal had to remain in Chinese hands.

"You must find the seal for me," the empress said.

Zhihao nearly chuckled. "This is the first time I am hearing of its disappearance. I have never read of this. I don't have even the slightest idea of where to begin looking. It could be anywhere."

"If I were to give you a clue, a key to finding it. If I could guarantee your success, would you do this task I have given you?"

He had to accept. No one could say no the empress. But he couldn't promise, even to himself, that he would hand over the seal if he found it. Maybe he would hide it again. Or perhaps he would find a Chinese leader worthy of it who could lead China in this new century. He would have to see what happened. But for now, he had no choice but to accept the assignment.

"I said that I would give my all in your service, Your Majesty," he said. "I stand by that. I will do my best to locate the emperor's seal."

The empress sat back in her throne and smiled. "Good," she said.

Why did he feel as though he had just made a pact with the devil?

"The clue?" he asked. "Or key? How am I to begin?"

The empress waved her hand and the door to the audience hall opened. In walked one of the most beautiful women he had ever seen.

Zhihao held his breath as she approached, as if she might disappear if he breathed. She was small with pale skin, though it was a bit darker than most palace ladies. She kept her eyes downcast and nearly floated as she took small steps and balanced on her high pot-bottom shoes that Manchu ladies wore. Her hair was wrapped around the high *batou* plank on top of her head but was simply adorned. Her floor-length *chaopao* was dark blue and embroidered with light blue flowers.

She stood next to Zhihao and got down on one knee in the half-kowtow position that was acceptable for ladies. Their ridiculous shoes made a full kowtow nearly impossible.

"Zhihao, meet the Lady Jiayi," the empress said.

Zhihao turned to her and bent at the waist in greeting. "My lady," he said.

She still did not look at him, but she nodded her acceptance.

"Jiayi," the empress said. "Tell him what you know about the seal."

"The seal was lost on the road to Jehol," she said in a soft voice. "The emperor and his family were traveling to the Mountain Palace when they were attacked by rebels. The emperor feared for his life and that the seal would be stolen. He entrusted it to Noble Lady Yi, the Lady Caigila. She was instructed to hide it, to keep it safe."

"If you can find out where that battle was," the empress explained, "the seal should be hidden nearby."

"How do you know this?" Zhihao asked Jiayi. "Did you find one of Lady Cai's letters or something?"

Jiayi shook her head. "No...I saw it...in a dream," she said.

Zhihao couldn't help but laugh. "Is this a joke?" he asked. One look at the empress told him that this was no joke. "I mean..." He quickly tried to save his skin. "I mean everyone has dreams from time to time of people we have met before or read about. How can you put any stock into some girl's dream about the seal?"

"You were instructed to bring an item with you, Zhihao. Something unique from your foreign travels. Did you?"

"Yes, Your Majesty," he said. He rummaged in his pockets until he found the item he had brought. It was a cameo brooch that had once been owned by Queen Elizabeth.

"Place it into Jiayi's hands," the empress instructed.

Jiayi delicately pulled the long sleeves of her robe up to her elbows and then held both of her hands in front of her. She closed her eyes and took a long, deep breath, as if she was steeling herself for something.

Zhihao felt his eyebrows scrunch in disbelief as he reached over and dropped the brooch into her hands.

Jiayi gasped and then slumped to the ground, as if she had fallen asleep.

Zhihao looked around, wondering if anyone should do anything to help her, but no one moved. Everyone seemed to be waiting with bated breath. The room remained silent for several minutes.

Finally, Jiayi's eyes shot open and she took a deep breath, as if she had not breathed the whole time she was in her sleep. She staggered back to her kneeling position.

"I was a queen," Jiayi said. "They called me Elizabeth. This jewel was a gift from her lover. She called him Dudley. He presented it to her at dinner, on the night of her coronation. The other people in the room did not look happy about it."

"Impossible!" Zhihao could not help but gasp. She was exactly right. He had researched the brooch extensively before purchasing it. But that was hardly the sort of thing a girl living in the Forbidden City would know. Zhihao snatched the brooch back from her. "This is...What is this? What is going on? Who is she?"

Several of the ladies in the room gasped, undoubtedly afraid he had angered the empress. But the empress only laughed. "Impressive, yes?"

"Yes...No! It's just not possible!" Zhihao stumbled.

"Why is it impossible? You saw it with your own eyes," the empress said. "She could not have known that. She never saw the thing before."

"But what is happening? What is going on? What does this have to do with the seal?"

"The girl is a seer," the empress said. "When she touches an item, she is transported to a time in the item's past, to the body of someone who interacted with the item. She can see events surrounding it."

"So...by touching the brooch she was able to see when the brooch was given to Queen Elizabeth?"

The empress nodded. "Now you are understanding," she said.

"But, what about the seal? How did she see it if the seal is lost?"

"I have the original box the seal was hidden in. She was able to see up to the moment the seal was removed from the box."

"And the seal was removed from the box by Lady Cai? On the road to Jehol?"

"Actually, the emperor removed the seal from the box

and handed it to Lady Cai. That was where my vision ended," Jiayi corrected.

"Wait." Zhihao closed his eyes and pinched the bridge of his nose. "I can't believe I'm actually engaging in this. It's crazy!"

Jiayi pursed her lips tightly and turned away. Zhihao felt a wave of guilt wash over him and he wondered just how many times the girl had been called crazy in her life. But she had to be crazy, or he was, or this was all some elaborate hoax.

"I just mean that this can't be real. There has to be an explanation for her visions. I can't go digging around in the dirt based on some girl's dream."

"Why not?" the empress asked. "There are things in this world that we cannot explain. This is one of them. But it is also one that can help you. Can help China! The court will pay all your expenses...and..."

Zhihao quirked an eyebrow. In all the excitement he had completely forgotten to ask about any remuneration for his work.

"Before he died, I believe you and Prince Gong talked about building a grand museum, like they have in England. Magnificent palaces that house and protect the country's treasures. Do this for me, and I will give you the authority and funds to build China's first museum."

"I'll do it!" Zhihao replied without a second thought.

THREE

*J*iayi didn't know whether to be glad or horrified. She was excited about the chance to get out of the palace and learn from Zhihao, but he was terribly rude and arrogant. That he called her crazy stung. For years people thought she was either crazy or possessed by a demon. If the empress hadn't taken her in when she did, who knows where Jiayi would have ended up. She shuddered to think of the possibilities.

"Very good," the empress said. "However, remember that your job and Jiayi's abilities must be kept secret. If the wrong people find out that the seal is missing, they could use that information against us. And if anyone outside this room knew what Jiayi could do, she could be in grave danger. She is precious to me. I want her back...in the exact same condition she is now."

The emphasis on the empress's final words made Jiayi blush.

"You mean...I am to take her with me?" Zhihao asked. "Has she not already told me all of what she saw?"

"She can still have more visions after she has rested. She

might see something useful later. But you can at least start figuring out where exactly you should be looking and start your journey."

The empress then stood to leave, and Jiayi and Zhihao bowed. They did not rise until she and her entourage had completely left the room. Then they stood and faced each other, but Jiayi kept her gaze to the floor. Even though she and Zhihao were mostly alone, it would not be proper for her to look him in the face. This was the first time in her life, in her real life, that she had ever been alone with a man —a real man at least. Eunuchs did not count as men. She glanced to the side of the room and saw that Eunuch Lo, her minder, had not left the room and was watching her from a discreet distance. She wondered if Zhihao knew he was even there.

Yet here she was about to travel and work with this man she had only just met. Her whole life was about to change, but she was too shy to say a thing. She hoped he would speak soon.

"Will you walk with me, Lady Jiayi?" he asked.

She gave a small bend of her knees to indicate her agreement. "If you like," she said in nearly a whisper, amazed she could speak at all.

He motioned toward the door. She walked outside first, but then he moved to her side as they walked down a garden path.

"So, tell me more about your...powers, Lady Jiayi," he said.

"Just 'Jiayi' is acceptable," she said. "The empress titled me 'lady' only to be polite, but I am no lady. I was born to a very poor family in one of the city's many *hutongs*."

"And are you Manchu?" he asked.

"I am," she said.

"And were you born with these abilities?" he asked as they turned down a path toward a koi pond.

"I believe so," she said, but that was an oversimplification of her past. She remembered the very first day she had a vision in stark clarity. But she did not feel the need to elaborate to this stranger. Perhaps later, if she thought she could trust him, she would reveal more. She looked into the rippling water, hoping to get a better look at his face, but the lighting was not quite right, so they both looked like dark blobs hovering over the darting fish. "I have had visions for as long as I can remember."

"How does it work?" he asked.

"You saw it," she said. "There is nothing more to it."

"There has to be more," he said. "Can you travel into anyone? Anytime? What about this pocket watch?" He pulled a fob watch out of his sleeve. Manchu style robes did not have pockets on the outside like Western-style clothes, but ones that were hidden more discretely, such as inside the large sleeves.

"I cannot do it all the time," she explained. She turned toward him and gently touched the watch, running her fingers over the silver of the round watch face. She then resumed walking. "The visions are...very taxing. I knew nothing would happen if I touched your watch just now. It can take hours, even days to recover, depending on how... emotionally charged a vision is.

"And I cannot control it. I don't know where I will go or who I will be. For example, the seal and the box that contained it are hundreds of years old. They have been touched by countless people, including half a dozen emperors. When I touch the seal, I could end up in any time and at any place. I have been jumping back into the seal's timeline for years. The empress is obsessed with it. My last vision, when I was Lady Cai, that was the closest I had ever gotten to when the seal was actually lost."

Zhihao nodded, taking all of this in. "So, you have been an emperor's lady. Have you been an emperor? That must be exciting for someone like you."

Someone like her? Jiayi wasn't sure what he meant by that, but she shook her head. "I have only ever jumped into a woman's body."

"And how long do the visions last?" he asked.

"Only as long as I can hold my breath," she said. "But over the years, I have learned to hold my breath for a very long time."

"Sounds quite dangerous," he said.

"There have been times when I was quite scared," she admitted. "Sometimes the people I jump into are in dangerous situations, in the middle of battles or on horse-back or standing on the edge of a cliff. I never know what to expect."

"Sounds like you have lived a very interesting life," he said.

She could not help but smile. "In my visions, yes," she said. "I was still quite young when I was given to the empress. And ever since, she has kept me under lock and key. I am grateful for her protection, for how she has provided me with food and security, but to her, I am little more essential than her Pekingese dogs—ornamental and occasionally entertaining. If I can find the seal, I will finally prove my worth to her. Then maybe she will let me be more than a kept pet."

She realized that Zhihao had stopped walking. She glanced up and saw that he was staring at her. She felt her face go hot. "I cannot believe I said those things!" she said. "Forgive me. I am so stupid. I...I should go..."

As she turned, she felt his grip on her elbow. "Stay," he said. She finally chanced a glance at his face, just for a moment. He was quite handsome, with smiling eyes and smooth lips. She did not allow her eyes to linger, though, since it would not be proper.

"You believe me now?" she dared to ask.

He laughed, an open and pleasant sound louder than any of his stifled snorts that escaped during the audience with the empress. "Well, you are entertaining if nothing else," he said.

The smile dropped from her face. What was wrong with this man? Every time she started to think he might not be completely terrible, he would say something else rude.

He seemed to notice her change in mood and quickly tried to placate her. "What I mean is, you are a brilliant storyteller. You should be a writer. You can write about all these fantastical visions you see."

Her shoulders dropped. What would he think of her if he knew she couldn't read or write? She already told him she was born to a poor family. He probably had no idea what that was like. She felt so stupid around him. He had traveled and been to a foreign university. He knew English and was friends with Prince Gong before his death. Without her visions, she would be nothing, just another dirty peasant living off scraps or a prostitute in a filthy flower house. She could never tell him these things, though. He already thought she was a fraud. She didn't have much, but she did have some dignity. She would hold onto what little she had.

"Sometimes I sketch the things I see," she said. "I'm not very good, of course, but the drawings help me remember."

"That's excellent," Zhihao said. "You will have to show me someday."

The two stood together in awkward silence for a moment, staring into the koi pond they had walked a complete circle around. Zhihao cleared his throat. "I can see I have upset you," he said. "Forgive me, I...this is all just so..."

"*Crazy?*" she spat.

"No," he said slowly. "I was going to say new. Simply... new. It is going to take some time to process. You must understand my point of view. In a world full of fake fortune tellers and astrologists, the idea that you can see the past... Well, it is hard to believe."

"So, because some fortune tellers are fake, then I must be fake too?" she asked rhetorically. Not giving him time to answer, she continued, "Perhaps you need a new perspective. If I am real, maybe some fortune tellers are too."

His jaw dropped, and she could not control the edges of her lips as they tugged upward. He then broke out into laughter again. "You...you, girl. You are, as the English would say, quite a *corker*."

"*Corker?*" she asked, trying to imitate his English.

"It's a compliment," he said. "Like brilliant."

"Can you teach me English?" she asked.

"I don't see why I can't teach you a few things," he said. "It will take us a while to travel the road to Jehol and back. And there will be plenty of evening time when it is too dark to search."

"And history?" she asked.

"You want to learn about history?" he asked.

She nodded. "Very much so," she said. "I always thought that if I knew more about history—the places, the people, the dress, the customs—I could better interpret my visions."

"I see," he said. "Well, I'm sure we will both learn a lot from each other over the next few weeks."

A slight breeze blew and she looked up and noticed the sun was high in the sky. "I should return to the empress," she said.

"Yes, of course," he said. He bowed at the waist, took her hand, and lightly kissed the back of it. Her hand was ensconced within her floor-length sleeves, so his lips did not actually touch her skin, but the mere act left her in a state of shock. Men and women never touched each other, in public at least. He froze, hovering over her hand as though he also realized his great blunder too late.

"For...forgive me," he stammered. "I...You know how sequestered Chinese women are. I rarely interact with them. I'm more accustomed to British women, and that is the gentlemanly way to say goodbye. I...I should just go," he said. He quickly dropped her hand and turned on his heels. He was heading the wrong way to exit the Forbidden City, but Jiayi was not about to call out to him to correct him. The last thing she wanted was to get his attention again.

She looked around the garden to see if anyone had seen what happened. Of course, she was nearly surrounded by people! Eunuchs and maids, working or just walking. Palace guards. Ministers. Then, of course, there was Eunuch Lo, hovering under a nearby tree. He was always watching. Jiayi shuddered. The empress would find out what happened long before Jiayi made it back to her. Zhihao was so confusing. He looked Chinse and he spoke Chinese, but he was also so...*foreign*. He seemed to know nothing about Chinese decorum, which was strange for a man of his stature. His parents should be ashamed.

But at the same time, he was so exciting. She had never known someone who had seen and done so much. She yearned to learn from him. Maybe there was more she could do with her life than just have visions for the empress.

Who was she kidding? The empress would never let her leave. She would spend her whole life as a trick pony on a golden chain.

FOUR

*Z*hihao walked away from Jiayi as fast as he could. What an idiot he was! Something about her made him completely forget his senses. Was he actually entertaining the idea that she was...what? A seer, as the empress called her? Maybe she was a reincarnated bodhisattva. Buddhist mysticism was full of stories of men and women with incredible powers. But if he actually believed for a second the girl was what she claimed, maybe he was the actual crazy one.

Outside the palace, he hailed a rickshaw to take him back to the university. A place of reason and logic. A calm place he could think and perhaps puzzle everything out. He needed to do some research on the Daoguang Emperor and see if he ever was attacked on the road to Jehol.

He also needed to figure out how Jiayi knew about the history of Queen Elizabeth's brooch. Cameos were common. Practically every European woman owned one. She couldn't have guessed that the brooch belonged to the right person, even if that person was Queen Elizabeth. It would have been a one in a million guess. The summons did tell him to bring a historical item with him, so the empress knew he would bring something. He had told several of his colleagues that he had been called before the empress. Had he told one of them he planned to take the brooch? That would explain everything.

He didn't like to think that Jiayi was a liar, though. In their private chat, she seemed sincere enough. And a little scared. Perhaps the empress was behind the whole charade and Jiayi was merely an unwitting pawn. There was something very innocent about her. She was still rather young, he thought. Perhaps not even twenty. But her eyes, large and dark, had a knowingness behind them. Possibly during her years of poverty, she learned more about the world than any child should. Or maybe after traveling into the bodies of women throughout time, she had already lived several lives.

Oh stop! he chided himself. It was simply ridiculous! He had to stop considering that the girl could really travel through time and space by touching an object. There had to be another explanation. The empress was privy to information about the court and emperors of old, information that would be kept secret from anyone who wasn't a member of the emperor's inner circle. She knew about the loss of the seal when there was no public knowledge of it. Perhaps she also knew that the emperor had given it to his consort during a battle.

But why the ruse with the girl? Why not just hire him to find the seal and command his secrecy? Why make up such an elaborate fantasy and involve Jiayi? And demand he take her with him on the search? Maybe she needed to send someone she could trust on the quest, someone who would report back faithfully.

It all made perfect sense. By the time he arrived back at the university, he was quite proud of himself for seeing through the empress's plan. Well, she'd have to try a lot harder to fool him. Looking back on the scene, how Jiayi and the empress pulled off their show was painfully obvious. Well, not that it mattered. Zhihao would find the seal and the empress would reward him with an endowment to build China's first museum.

If he handed the seal over. The fact that the Manchu had been ruling China without the Mandate of Heaven for decades angered him. Maybe the seal should just stay lost. Or stay in the hands of a true Han Chinese. After three hundred years, it was time for the Chinese to govern themselves.

"Hey!" He felt a hand clap him on the back just as he arrived at the library.

"What?" Zhihao asked, startled.

"Sleepwalking?" his friend Lian asked him with a laugh. "I've been talking to you for like five minutes! It's like you were in a trance."

Zhihao snorted a bit at that. "I do feel like I just walked out of an imaginary world," he said.

"Oh, right!" his friend said. "You were at the Forbidden City this morning! What was it like?"

"Unbelievable," Zhihao said. "By the way, who else knew I was going? I told you and Hu Xiaosheng and Dr. Bennett, the chancellor. Did you tell anyone?"

"I'm sure I did," he said. "You going to see the empress is the most exciting thing to happen to me in months."

Zhihao wrinkled his nose. Everyone on campus probably knew he had been summoned to the empress. Tracking down whoever told her about the brooch might be impossible. He would have to be more discreet in the future.

"Did you mention the cameo?" Zhihao asked.

"What cameo?" Lian replied.

"The empress told me to bring a unique item with me in the summons. I took Queen Elizabeth's brooch. Did you mention that to anyone else?"

"I didn't know about that," Lian said. "I mean, I know you were told to bring something, but when I last saw you, you hadn't decided what to take. You took the brooch? What did she think?"

Lian was one of his best friends, so he didn't think he would lie to him. Maybe he just forgot if he had told anyone about it.

"She was quite fascinated by it," Zhihao lied. "Anyway, I need to do some research—"

"Aren't you going to tell me what happened? What did she want?"

"Unfortunately, I have been sworn to secrecy, my friend. She'd probably lop my head off if I told you."

"No way!" his friend said with a laugh. "Every bit the dragon lady, yeah?"

"You could say that," Zhihao said. He reached into his sleeve to check the time on his pocket watch, but he couldn't find it. He checked his other pockets, but turned up nothing. He must not have secured it properly after showing it to Jiayi and dropped it by the pond. He would have to ask her later if she found it. "Do you have the time? I seem to have misplaced my watch. I hate how bilious these sleeves are."

"It's only around noon," Lian said. "I need to get to class."

"Sure. We'll talk later, okay?"

"I know you'll tell me more after a bottle of *baijiu* tonight," Lian called out as he walked away.

Zhihao bounded up the stairs of the building that held

the main library. Hu Xiaosheng was sure to be there. He was rarely anywhere else. Hu Xiaosheng was not a historian in the modern sense; he didn't do field research or collect information from old texts. Hu Xiaosheng was living history. Eighty years if he was a day, Hu Xiaosheng was descended from a long line of village storytellers. He was a living example of the old world oral tradition. One of Zhihao's jobs at the university was to transcribe Hu Xiaosheng's stories onto paper before they were lost. Even though Zhihao doubted that some of the things Hu Xiaosheng told him were true, and most of his stories could never be verified by any existing written texts, Zhihao loved the impassioned way Hu Xiaosheng expressed himself. Sometimes Zhihao would forget that he was supposed to be writing and would just get lost in the tales. He had no idea if Hu Xiaosheng would know anything about the missing seal, but he was as good a place to start as any.

The Peking University Library was a large modern building three stories tall. Hu Xiaosheng was usually on the first floor, all the way in the back of the building, surrounded by dusty scrolls and tomes as old as he was. Even though he was an oral historian, he loved reading and had a fantastic memory. He was often able to recall even the most obscure of facts.

Zhihao ambled down the long aisles that were crammed with old books and random relics of history. Old wooden puppets, decorative door carvings, a jade dragon, bronze urns containing the remains of the long forgotten dead.

Zhihao found Hu Xiaosheng where he expected to, mumbling to himself as he poured over an ancient document. Zhihao speculated that Hu Xiaosheng's incessant mumbling, which he always did as he read, was part of the reason his memory was so good.

"Greetings, Hu Xiaosheng," Zhihao said with a respectful bow, using the honorific title for teacher.

Hu Xiaosheng waved him off and barely looked up from his reading. "So, how did your meeting with the empress go?" he asked.

"So direct," Zhihao observed.

"At my age, you don't waste time," Hu Xiaosheng said.

"Indeed," Zhihao replied. "It was...interesting, to be certain. Do you know anything about the emperor's seal?"

"You mean the one that was lost?"

Zhihao's jaw dropped, and not for the first time that day. He quickly rubbed his chin to try and compensate. He seemed to be the only person who *didn't* know the seal had been missing.

"How...how do you know that?" Zhihao asked.

"I know things," Hu Xiaosheng said. "Sometimes I just forget what I know until I remember it."

"Any idea where you learned about the seal?"

Hu Xiaosheng shook his head. "It was hidden in the back of my mind somewhere. I just know that when the Daoguang Emperor took the throne, he had the seal. But when his son, the Xianfeng Emperor, came to power, the seal was gone. Some people think it was lost during the Opium War. That maybe the British have it hidden away."

"That could be a possibility, I suppose," Zhihao said. "But the empress doesn't think so. She seems to think it was lost on the road to Jehol, on one of the emperor's trips to the Mountain Palace."

"Why would she think that?" Hu Xiaosheng asked, finally looking up from his papers.

Zhihao thought it was best not to mention Jiayi if possible. He didn't want to lose face in front of his teacher by admitting he nearly fell for a charlatan's cheap parlor trick.

"She says there was a battle on the road. Some rebel group attacked the travelers, so the emperor thought it was best to hide the seal, to prevent the rebels from getting their hands on it."

"So why didn't he go back and get it after it was safe?" Hu Xiaosheng asked.

"As you said, Xiaosheng, it was lost," Zhihao said.

Hu Xiaosheng nodded his head slowly and seemed to mull this over for a moment. "You know," he finally said, "the Daoguang Emperor loved his Mountain Palace, and was rather a fool for governance. Why else would he appoint Xianfeng as his heir? That witless boy. Anyone else could have seen that Prince Gong should have been his heir."

Zhihao nodded in agreement. Even though doubting the decisions of the emperor was tantamount to treason, now that the Daoguang Emperor, the Xianfeng Emperor, and Prince Gong were all dead, the old game of "what would have happened if Prince Gong had been emperor" was a favorite among scholars and even laypersons interested in China's past, present, and future. Especially among revolutionaries.

"He ran away from his responsibilities as often as possible. He would go to the Mountain Palace every chance he got, three or four times a year...until...hmm..."

"Until what?" Zhihao prompted.

Hu Xiaosheng wandered away, down an aisle between some of the shelves. He scanned them, looking for something. Zhihao didn't bother to ask for more information. He knew that Hu Xiaosheng would tell him when he found what he was looking for, so he just followed along.

Looking up and down the crowded shelves, Hu Xiaosheng mumbled to himself. He finally came across a pile of scrolls, all of which looked the same to Zhihao, and pulled a few out. He then walked over to a large table and spread them out, occasionally licking one of his fingers to more easily grip the dry pages.

"There is no mention of the Daoguang Emperor and his family being set upon while on the road to Jehol. But there was something odd about one trip..." He flipped a few more pages, looking for a specific passage. "Ah! Here," he said, pointing at what seemed to be little more than a travel record.

"Record of the journey to Jehol, Autumn, in the fourteenth year of the reign of the Daoguang Emperor..." Zhihao read. He quickly calculated in his head what year that would have been according to the Gregorian calendar and came up with 1834, almost seventy years ago.

"Day one, arrived safely at first camp in the midafternoon. The emperor took his leisure in his tent with several ladies..." Food, hunting, entertainment, rest—all regular activities for an imperial procession to the Mountain Palace. But on day three, the procession seemed to stop. The group rested for five days, which was indeed highly abnormal.

"The trip to Jehol was usually only seven days," Hu Xiaosheng said. "Why would they suddenly stop halfway there and rest for five days with no explanation? The record then carries on as normal, eating, hunting, and so on. There is no explanation for why they stayed in one place for five days. If one of the children or ladies had taken ill, the scribe could have simply said so. Why the mystery?"

"Why, indeed," said Zhihao. "You think this long break could have been when the battle was staged and the seal lost?"

"It's as good a theory as any," Hu Xiaosheng said. "After this, the emperor's visits to Jehol dropped dramatically. He didn't return for over two years, and when he did resume his visits, they were less frequent, only one or two trips a year. And his protection doubled. It was like traveling with an army."

"He was perhaps paranoid of being attacked on the road again," Zhihao said. "Three days out...that would have only been about ninety *li* from the city. What's out there? Isn't there a narrow part of the trail through there?"

Hu Xiaosheng nodded. "The Conghua Pass."

"The Conghua Pass!" Zhihao repeated. "Of course! The pass would be an excellent place for an army to attack."

"Sounds like you have a good place to start your search," Hu Xiaosheng said, turning back to his readings.

"Thank you for your assistance, Hu Xiaosheng," Zhihao said respectfully before he turned to leave.

At first, Hu Xiaosheng did not acknowledge him, but when Zhihao was halfway out of the room, he said one last thing.

"By the way," the voice cracked in a low tone, "be careful of trusting that girl. Such power should not be taken lightly."

Zhihao whirled back around. "How...? You couldn't have read that or heard about it from someone else so quickly. I came right here after my meeting. What do you know about the girl?"

"Just what I said," was all Hu Xiaosheng said as he returned to his manuscripts.

Hu Xiaosheng did seem to know something about everything. Zhihao reasoned that it was possible the old man knew that the empress had a seer of some sort in her employ. But how did he know that Zhihao had met her? He knew that asking would do no good. Hu Xiaosheng only shared what he wanted when he wanted, and the fact that he had turned back to his manuscripts told Zhihao that he wouldn't get anything else out of the old man today. He grabbed a few books on his way out about the Daoguang Emperor and the Mountain Palace. He still needed to know more about the emperor, Lady Cai, and the Conghua Pass if he had any chance of finding the seal.

FIVE

*L*ate that night, long after the rest of the Forbidden City had fallen asleep, Jiayi was wide awake. She held the chain of Zhihao's pocket watch with a handkerchief and slowly swayed the fob back and forth. She had told him she grew up poor, but she had not told him just how poor. That she had become a thief, a pickpocket, to survive. She had easily slipped the watch from his sleeve without him noticing when he kissed her hand. Even in her state of shock, she had no problem sliding the watch into her other hand. Her life needing to thieve to survive was now far behind her, but some habits were hard to let go of. She knew that one day she would outlive her usefulness to the empress, then what would happen to her? She couldn't help stealing small items here and there, things she could later sell if she needed to. Maybe she could even sell them and earn enough money before the empress kicked her out. That way, she could leave the palace on her own terms. She could sneak out in the night, sell the pilfered items, and hop a ship to America. She had heard that there were jobs in America for young ladies, jobs as housemaids and seamstresses. She didn't know much about cleaning or sewing, but she would be willing to learn.

Jiayi finally slipped silently from her bed. She had a room to herself, but it was small and the window was uncovered. Eunuch Lo had been assigned by the empress to watch Jiayi night and day, and he was currently stationed outside her bedroom door. By this time of night, though, he had most certainly fallen asleep. Jiayi didn't trust Eunuch Lo. She was certain that he had seen her steal one of the empress's combs years ago, but he never reported her. She did not know why. Was he waiting to use that knowledge against her later? She was too afraid of him to ask why he did not report her, but not scared enough to stop stealing.

Jiayi's room was little more than a closet. She had a small bed near a fireplace and a trunk for her few clothes, shoes, and hair decorations. She opened her trunk and removed one of her hairpins. She then used the pin to lift a loose floorboard, revealing a hole in the ground. In the hole was Jiayi's horde of stolen items. Hairpins, pieces of embroidery, gold coins, even some of the empress's jewelry. She could be put to death for stealing any one of the items, much less the whole cache of them. She placed Zhihao's pocket watch among the other items and pulled out something wrapped in a piece of cloth. She hopped back into her bed, pulling her blanket over her lap. She gingerly unwrapped the cloth and revealed a gold necklace.

The necklace was exquisite. It was a piece of traditional wedding jewelry. On one side was a phoenix and the other a dragon. The two met in the middle, where there was the character for eternal happiness. The character was embellished with swirls of gold and a large red ruby dangled from the center of the character.

Jiayi shouldn't be doing this. She needed to preserve her

strength to search for the lost seal. But she couldn't resist. She needed to see him. His soul called to hers through the centuries.

She took a deep breath and quickly clasped the necklace around her neck before she slumped to the side.

Jiayi could hear the drumming of hoofbeats before she opened her eyes. She felt something in her hands and clenched her fists. She heard the roar of the crowd and felt herself move up and down, up and down. When she opened her eyes, she was on horseback. She lowered herself to find her balance and gripped the reins in one hand and the polo mallet in the other. She squinted in the bright sunshine and saw the small white ball just ahead of her. She leaned to the side and whacked the ball as hard as she could down the field. The crowd hollered and cheered. She could not help but smile as she continued chasing the ball. Other riders—men and women—came up beside her, either hoping to help move the ball down the field or to steal it and knock it the other direction. She had no idea who was on her team, but win or lose, she loved the excitement of riding the horse and competing. By her time period, women were not allowed to participate in such masculine activities. But now, during the Tang Dynasty, women were given much more freedom.

A male rider swooped in front of her and blocked another rider from reaching the ball. She used his guard to lean over and smack the ball farther down the field. A fellow woman rider cut across her path and hit the ball, knocking it into the goal. The crowd jumped and screamed, and she laughed. The men on her team bowed their heads at her for her excellent performance. The woman who had scored the winning goal rode to her side and embraced her.

"Excellent job, Lady Meirong," the woman said.

"That was a thrilling match," Jiayi replied, her smile huge.

The riders all galloped to the edge of the field and were helped from their horses and given drinks. Jiayi looked around anxiously. She only had a minute or two left before she would run out of breath. She had to see him. Someone handed her a wet cloth to clean herself with. She used it on her face, neck, and hands as she walked toward the tent of the imperial family. Just as she was about to enter, a hand grasped hers and pulled her to the side.

Prince Junjie—the man she had traveled through time and risked the wrath of the empress to see—put his finger to her lips to make sure she didn't cry out. She stifled a giggle as they ran behind the tent.

"You played magnificently," he said.

"You are too kind," she said. "It was Lady Lin who scored the win."

"You look terrible," he said with a joking smile. And oh, what a smile. His lips were slightly pink and so smooth. His cheeks dimpled and his eyes sparkled. He was the most handsome man she had ever seen in real life or in all her dreams.

She gasped and put her hand to her head. Indeed, her cloudy chignon was a rat nest and she pulled out a piece of straw. Her long gown was filthy. She could only imagine how her face looked.

"Not all of us can sit aside in the empress's tent and be fanned by slaves," she said.

"What I wouldn't give for you to sit by my side," he said with a sigh.

She looked down. She knew this part of the story. It was always the same. Prince Junjie was a third son of the late emperor's brother. A warrior. A scholar. A man destined for greatness. Lady Meirong was a niece of the empress. She was a lady, yes, but not one high ranking enough to marry a prince. She would most likely be married to a general or a low-ranking magistrate, if she were lucky. At seventeen, she was already getting too old to make a good match. Prince Junejie and Lady Meirong knew they could never be together, so they savored the little time they did have.

Jiayi wasn't even sure if Meirong loved the prince or was just enjoying his attention. But Jiayi loved him with every beat of her heart. She had loved him from the first time she saw him after traveling with the amulet several years before. She would do anything for him. She had stolen the amulet for him so she could travel to him whenever she wanted. She couldn't live without him. Her real life at the empress's court was so miserable, the only happiness she knew was the few moments she could steal away in the night to find Prince Junjie. It was dangerous—she was risking her life. If the empress knew she had stolen the amulet, she could be put to death. If she spent so much of her energy traveling to see the prince that she did not have the power to travel for the empress, the empress could simply discard her. The empress had no time or patience for a useless mystic.

But she couldn't stop herself. She had to be near him. She truly believed that fate had separated her from her true love by centuries. And he didn't even know her name.

"Please," she said, realizing their time was short. "No time for sadness. Just love me now."

He leaned in and pressed his lips to hers. His kisses at first were gentle, but she wanted—*needed*—more. She wrapped her arms around his neck and pulled him tight. She tangled her fingers in his long thick hair and he moaned when she gave a tug. He pushed her up against the wall of the tent and nibbled at her chin, then her neck. He ran his hand around her backside and she gasped.

"I love you," she whispered as she felt him start to slip away from her. "Never forget that. Never forget me."

Her eyes shot open and she had to stifle a cry. She put her hands to her chest and breathed slowly and steadily in and out. Then the tears came. Every time she was ripped away from Prince Junjie, she felt a part of her heart break. She forced her hand to her mouth so her crying would not wake her eunuch guard. She removed the necklace and wrapped it back in the simple cloth. She crept to the floor and placed it back in its hiding place. Exhausted from her journey, she crawled back into bed and quickly fell asleep.

SIX

The next day, Jiayi was taken before the empress nearly after dawn, as was usual, by Eunuch Lo. The empress had always been an early riser. What surprised her, though, was that Zhihao was also present. She bent at the knees to greet him. He nodded at her with a smile.

"I am very pleased with the progress Zhihao Shaoye has made," the empress said.

Jiayi noticed the respectful way the empress referred to Zhihao. She must have been happy with him indeed.

"Tell Lady Jiayi what you have told me," the empress commanded.

Zhihao turned to her. "Well, I could not find any information about a battle on the road to Jehol," he explained. Jiayi felt her stomach drop a little. This gave him more reason to doubt her abilities. "However," he continued, "there was a strange incident. On one journey, there was an exceptionally long delay at the Conghua Pass. There was no explanation for the delay, no illness or anything by any of the party members. It could be that the delay was caused by an attack, but it was stricken from the record to prevent people from finding out and panicking. Or to hide the loss of the seal."

Jiayi smiled, glad that he was able to affirm her vision even though there was no record of it. "That is wonderful," she said. "I am glad you have a lead. Hopefully it will be easy to find now."

Zhihao chuckled a little. "The Conghua Pass is still a large area. And who knows if the seal stayed in the pass or if it was moved..." He shook his head. "It is a lead, yes, but this is only the beginning of the search."

Jiayi nodded. "The task ahead is still quite difficult, it sounds."

"Indeed," Zhihao confirmed. "Which is why I think the empress's idea of sending you on the expedition is an excellent one."

Jiayi's heart leaped, but she did her best to keep her face calm. She wanted to leave the Forbidden City more than anything, but she could not let the empress think she was ungrateful for being taken off the street and provided for.

Jiayi nodded. "I will go where the empress bids me."

"Good," the empress said. "You will go with Zhihao. Eunuch Lo will accompany you."

Jiayi did her best to conceal a grimace. She could go nowhere and do nothing without Eunuch Lo's knowledge or approval. Even now, she could almost feel his eyes boring into the back of her. She had been hoping that if the empress let her leave the Forbidden City with Zhihao, she would also allow her to leave Eunuch Lo behind. But she realized that leaving the Forbidden City was more than she could have hoped for. Leaving Eunuch Lo behind as well was more than she should have dared dream.

"Of course," Jiayi finally said with a nod of her head.

"And you, Zhihao Shaoye," the empress continued. "You said that you needed assistants. I understand you will need men to carry your goods. And you have requested some of your fellow historians to travel with you. You do realize how sensitive this issue is, do you not? If the wrong people hear about the lost seal, the entire empire could be in danger."

"I realize that, Your Majesty," Zhihao said. "But this task is large. We will need all manner of equipment. And a translator, since the people around Conghua speak a different dialect. A geographer would be helpful as well. There are hills and caves and rivers around Conghua. If we don't know the terrain, it could be very dangerous. And other people familiar with the Daoguang Emperor to share ideas with and help with research would be useful. I estimate a party of fifty people should be sufficient for an expedition such as this."

"*Fifty people?*" the empress spat. Jiayi wasn't sure if the empress was going to laugh or scream. "This is a *secret* expedition, you fool. You will complete this expedition with three people—yourself, Lady Jiayi, and Eunuch Lo."

"*What?*" Zhihao nearly yelled back before he remembered who he was addressing. Jiayi could almost see Zhihao physically biting his lip to keep from correcting the empress. One did not correct the empress if he valued his head upon his shoulders.

"You accepted the task of finding the seal. Do you still believe you can find it? Are you capable, Long Zhihao?" she demanded, using his family name for emphasis.

He nodded, but he fidgeted with his hat in his hands. Jiayi could see he was swallowing his words and his pride.

"I will find the seal, Your Majesty," he finally said aloud. "You will not be disappointed."

"Good," the empress said. "You will leave at first light

tomorrow." She stood, and Jiayi and Zhihao knocked their foreheads to the floor. They did not rise until the empress and her ladies had left the room.

When they sat up again, Zhihao's face was red. Jiayi did not know if it was from anger or from holding his face to the floor. She hoped it was the latter but was reasonably certain it was the former. She felt the need to say something, to placate him in some way, yet she did not know this man well enough to temper his moods.

"This is a fool's errand," Zhihao finally said through clenched teeth in a low voice.

Jiayi looked at him sharply, her eyes wide. "But you said—"

"What else was I supposed to say?" he snapped, then his eyes darted around the room and he saw Eunuch Lo watching them. He took a breath and lowered his voice before continuing. "When I accepted the job yesterday, I didn't think to ask how many men I would be able to take with me. I thought that whatever I needed would be at my disposal. I didn't consider that she would handicap me with a eunuch and a woman."

He stood up and stomped out of the audience chamber, apparently sure he had gotten the last word in.

Jiayi felt her own anger rise up. She should have expected nothing less from someone so infuriating. She got to her feet and followed him out of the building and down the stairs.

"You would not have a chance at finding the seal at all if not for this *woman*," she yelled. He turned back and looked at her with a scowl on his face. "If we find the seal, it will be because of *me*. If you get your museum, it will be because of *me*."

"Drop the act," Zhihao said with an exasperated sigh.

"We all know your visions are nothing but an elaborate show."

"What?" she asked. After her demonstration yesterday, she thought he believed in her, at least a little bit. That he now completely doubted her was shocking and upsetting.

"There is a perfectly good explanation for all of this," he said. "Of course the empress would know the seal was missing. She has access to imperial archives that no one else does. She could have known about the battle at Conghua Pass even though there is no record anywhere else. And she could have a spy at the university. She has spies everywhere else. She could have known ahead of time that I was bringing Queen Elizabeth's brooch. It all makes sense."

"What about me?" she asked. "If there is an explanation for the rest of it, why am I here?"

"Who knows?" he said. "The empress could just be—" He stopped himself.

Jiayi narrowed her eyes and leaned toward him. "Say it," she dared him.

Zhihao paused and looked up, probably rifling through his mental thesaurus. "Eccentric," he finally settled on.

Jiayi gritted her teeth. Eccentric was the same as crazy, but for rich people. He didn't believe her, and what's worse, he didn't believe the empress. If he didn't believe, would he even try to find the seal? Was this a holiday for him? At least if he didn't find it, he wouldn't be any worse off than he was now. But what about her? They had to find the seal if she hoped to stay in the empress's good graces. Her hope for a better future depended on him, but he didn't seem very dependable right now.

She wanted to yell and scream. Tell him how mean he was and how he was putting her life at risk. But Jiayi had learned a long time ago that it was her powers that would save her. She had to depend on herself for her survival. She reached over and took a pin from his hat, one she had noticed he always wore even if the hat was different. She took a short shallow breath because she didn't want to be gone for long. She only needed to gather enough information to prove she was real.

When she opened her eyes, she was sitting at a table across from Zhihao. It was daylight and they were in what looked like a large dining hall, but there were lots of tables and lots of people...lots of white people. Zhihao was the only Chinese man in the room. She looked at her hands and realized she too was white. She reached up and pulled down a strand of hair. Blonde curly hair. She had to be in England, maybe London, back when Zhihao was studying there.

"It's gorgeous," he said, holding up the pin she was holding in real life. "You are too sweet, Rebecca." He reached across and took her pale hand in his tawny one. "This has been a wonderful birthday."

She smiled sweetly and did her best not to recoil at his touch. "I only want you to be happy," she said.

He frowned and looked pensive. "You know I love you, Rebecca," he said.

Jiayi felt her eyes widen. Thankfully he was looking at her hand and not her face. He loved her? A foreigner? How ludicrous! But how should she respond? Did Rebecca love him back? She couldn't tell, and she didn't have much time to figure it out.

"Of course...darling..." she forced herself to say.

"But I cannot take you with me. My parents would never allow it. Even if we married here, they would not recognize you once we arrived back in China. I'm sorry."

She was stuck between Rebecca's intense emotions and

her own anger. She could feel that Rebecca wanted to burst into tears. Her heart was breaking. But Jiayi was incensed. Of course his parents would reject such a match. It was ridiculous. He would have to marry a girl of his choosing. He should submit to his parents' will.

She finally settled for a compromise. She allowed some tears to escape, but she would not wail and cause a scene. As a few tears leaked from her eyes, she looked around and noticed many of the other people were already watching them. In London, a Chinese man and a white woman together must have seemed just as shocking as it would in Peking.

"I...I understand," she said, giving the safe answer. She picked up a napkin and dabbed the tears from her cheeks with it. "You must respect your parents."

He chuckled. "You don't believe that any more than I do," he said. "I want to marry you, take to you China, but... it's more than my parents, it's the whole society, the whole culture. You would never be accepted. You would never be happy."

"I'd never be happy without you," Jiayi blurted out, and her tears fell a little harder. She must have been losing her control over Rebecca. She would probably wake up any second. "Is this really about me? Or is it about him? You've never forgiven yourself for Eli's death."

"Rebecca, please," he said, shaking his head, nearly to tears himself. He pulled his hands away and lowered his voice to a whisper. "Don't do this. Don't bring him up. This is only about us, I swear."

"I'm sorry," she said.

"Maybe someday I can come back to you," he said. "I'll write you every week. We would at least stand a better chance here than in China."

"I'll wait for you..." she said as her vision blurred.

Jiayi gasped as she woke up. She was lying on the grass under the shade of a tree. Zhihao must have caught her as she fell and carried her here. Speaking of Zhihao, she glanced around and finally saw him. He was sitting near her, looking at her, but not with the eyes of love she just saw. He still looked angry.

She sat up. "Do you still write to her every week?" she asked.

Zhihao put his hand to his mouth, stifling a gasp. He ripped the pin away from her and put it back in his hat.

"No," he said, looking ashamed. "I...I was foolish. Just an idiot boy."

"You broke her heart, you know. The day she gave you that pin."

He stared at her, deep in her eyes, as if he was trying to see Rebecca there. She wondered if he saw her. She had seen through Rebecca's eyes, had felt what Rebecca felt. Did Rebecca feel anything of her?

"I...always wondered about that," Zhihao finally said. "I know we cared for each other, but how much we really loved each other is anyone's guess. We were stupid. The idea that we could be together was just..."

Jiayi raised an eyebrow at him.

"Yes," he said. "I was crazy. We were crazy. You..." He shook his head. "You are not crazy. There is no way you could have known that. I've never told anyone here about her." He paused and then asked, "Do you know her name?" He was giving her one last test.

"Reb...Rebka," Jiayi said, knowing she was saying it wrong but hoping it was close enough.

Zhihao nodded. "Rebecca," he said. "She never...hmm. Never mind. I shouldn't tell you anything more. It's not your problem." He stood up and straightened his clothes. She followed suit.

He was right. It wasn't Jiayi's problem, but she couldn't help but be curious. She wondered what she would learn from his pocket watch...

"Pack your things," he said. "We will leave tomorrow at dawn."

"So, you believe me?" she asked, hope swelling in her chest.

"I..." He paused, as if searching for the right words. "I shouldn't, but I can't deny what you saw. The rational part of my brain is saying that this isn't possible. But Rebecca... How could you know that? Even if the empress had been spying on me while I was away, you were too specific. You know too much. I don't know what is going on, but I will do my best to give you the benefit of the doubt."

"That is all I can ask," she replied.

SEVEN

The next morning, Zhihao was ready and excited to go. He had packed all the equipment he could imagine they would need for both living and working outdoors for several weeks—maps, tents, ropes, pickaxes, shovels, grappling hooks, brushes, buckets, cooking utensils —and was eager to get started.

Zhihao prepared three horses and a pack mule, but it had been a while since he had ridden a horse. Horses were not common pets or means of conveyance in China. He actually rode horses far more often when he was in England than while he was living in China. He was worried that Jiayi would not be able to ride a horse. Why would she? But she was even more eager for this trip than he was. He was sure she would be willing to learn if necessary.

When he arrived at the west gate of the Forbidden City, Jiayi and Eunuch Lo were waiting for him. Jiayi was smiling and nearly bouncing on her pot-bottom shoes. *Pot-bottom shoes?* Zhihao nearly wanted to yell. *What was she thinking?*

"You aren't going to be wearing that, are you?" Zhihao asked her, and the smile ran away from her face.

"What do you mean?" she asked.

Zhihao held out his arms to demonstrate proper expedition attire. He was wearing a white cotton shirt that buttoned down the front, khaki pants, a brown, wide-brimmed hat, and heavy black boots. Jiayi was still dressed as a court lady in a floor-length *chaopao*, her hair wrapped around a *batou*, and pot-bottomed shoes.

Eunuch Lo was not dressed much better, with his simple robe and cloth-soled shoes.

Jiayi shifted on her feet and stammered. "I don't own anything else."

"This simply won't do. You can barely walk in those shoes, much less go climbing around on rocks and in caves."

"What am I to do?" she asked.

Zhihao sighed, annoyed. But he wasn't sure who he should be annoyed with. Anyone should know that she couldn't go dressed like that, but what Chinese woman ever wore anything else? How was she to know?

"Very well," he said. "Let's find a rickshaw for you and you can follow me."

Jiayi nodded as Eunuch Lo went to the street and hailed a rickshaw. Zhihao yelled an address to the rickshaw puller. He led the horses and mule to a shop very near the Foreign Legation, which ran along the south wall of the Forbidden City. The Foreign Legation was where almost all foreign citizens residing in Peking lived. There were people of all nationalities living there, but mainly British, American, French, Russian, German, Belgian, Dutch, and Japanese. The Foreign Legation was its own city, but the area around the legation also catered to foreign tastes. The shop Zhihao had in mind was a dress shop.

Zhihao and Jiayi entered the shop to many staring eyes

while Eunuch Lo waited outside by the door. Zhihao addressed the shop owner, a Chinese woman, in English.

"Good day, madam," he said. "We are going exploring in the countryside and my female friend here needs some proper attire."

The woman was Chinese, but she carried herself like a foreigner. She was tall and held her head high. Her hair was curled and piled on her head and she wore a corseted gown.

Zhihao could not help but notice Jiayi cover her mouth in shock. He assumed she had never seen a woman dressed in such a way before, at least not in real life. But she had to have seen them in her visions.

The shopkeeper looked both of them up and down, at least as well as she could from behind her nose, which she held aloft, and then made her determination. Apparently, Zhihao's fine English had won her over.

"What exactly are you looking for, sir?" she asked.

"Something practical," he said. "Something for walking in, something that won't show dirt."

"Believe it or not," she said, "but I have just the thing." She went to a rack and rifled through it for a moment. "You wouldn't believe how many young women stuck over here are suddenly struck with the idea they want to run off on expeditions and have grand adventures. Their parents must be appalled, but what can you expect? These ladies have none of the comforts or confinements of home. They should just all stay back in London..." She droned on to herself as she found just the outfit. "Ah! Here it is. This girl is quite small, so the outfit will have to be taken in a bit, but I think it is just what you are looking for."

Zhihao nodded his approval. The ensemble was a corseted brown top that buttoned down the front and a brown pair of pants that had legs wide enough to almost look like a skirt. All Jiayi would need to complete the outfit was a pair of boots and a hat to protect her from the sun. He turned to Jiayi and explained in Chinese that the woman would help her dress in something more appropriate.

Jiayi hesitated and looked nervous, but eventually she followed the shop owner into another room to change. After several minutes, the owner returned.

"I'm sorry, sir," she said. "But the girl refuses to come out. She says she won't wear the top in public."

"Why?" he asked. "What's wrong with it?"

"She says it's indecent," she explained with a sigh.

Zhihao chuckled. "Nothing of the sort! It looked lovely."

"Try as you might, sir," she said. "I could not convince her."

Zhihao sighed and tapped on the door. "Jiayi," he said. "What's wrong?"

"I can't wear this outfit," she replied softly from the other side. "It's not proper."

"What is wrong with it?" he asked. "She can make adjustments so it fits better, if you need."

"The whole style is wrong," she said. "It just isn't right."

"What are you on about?" he asked. "Here, let me see."

"No!" she gasped. "That wouldn't be right!"

"Are you wearing the clothes?" he asked.

"Yes..." she said.

"Then I need to see what the problem is. I can't help you if you don't let me see."

She didn't reply, but after a moment he heard the click of the lock. He opened the door and couldn't help but gasp when he saw her. She looked amazing. The corset cinched in her tiny waist and propped up her small chest, giving her a rather desirable bosom. The legs of the pants were straight, but they still hugged her bottom. Her hair, which was usually tightly wrapped around the *batou*, was long and free. He'd never seen a Chinese woman dressed this way before and she took his breath away.

"What...umm...hum...what's wrong with it?" he finally stammered.

She crossed her arms over her chest as though to hide herself from his gaze. "Everything!" she said. "I can't wear this in public! It's indecent!"

"Come now," he said. "British women dress like this all the time. Not the pants so much, but a very similar skirt. Would you rather wear a skirt?"

"No!" she said. "I can't wear any of it. I can't let men see...me," she said. "I feel...exposed and just...wrong..."

Zhihao could see that she was near to tears and realized he was the person in the wrong. Even though European women were not afraid of showing—and emphasizing—their curves, for a Chinese woman it was nearly an inconceivable thought. Chinese *chaopaos* covered a woman from her neck to her feet and were long and straight. Chinese *men* wore clothes that fight tighter than women did. For her curves to be visible would be nearly the same as being naked to her. It was too much for him to ask of her.

"Very well," he said. Give me a moment. He left the shop and went to a Chinese tailor down the road. He picked out some more practical clothes for Eunuch Lo and returned to the ladies' shop with a man's *chaopao*, but a very simple dark cotton one. He handed it to Jiayi. "Take off the top and wear this. Tell me what you think."

She did as she was told and after some back and forth with the shopkeeper they finally arrived at a compromise. She would wear the man's top, but have the sleeves shortened. The *chaopao* itself was shortened to her calves, had slits up the sides, and was taken in some at the waist. She kept the brown wide-legged pants. The shopkeeper also found her a wide-brimmed hat. Jiayi wore her hair in a long braid down the back like Zhihao. She finished the look with a pair of heavy black boots. Zhihao had never seen anything so ridiculous and yet incredibly charming in his life.

It wasn't the obviously feminine look that Zhihao had hoped for, but at least Jiayi didn't look like a boy either. Her clothing was both perfectly acceptable and practical for the occasion. Zhihao bought her several sets of clothes since they had no idea how long they would be gone. She topped off the pile of clothes with a pair of brown gloves, and he nodded his understanding. With the shortened sleeves, her hands would be exposed. She needed some sort of protection to keep her from falling into a vision whenever she touched something new.

Jiayi was obviously happy with the clothes as well. She didn't simply accept that she had to wear them, but her face beamed. She couldn't stop smiling. In her new outfit, she gripped her horse's reigns and climbed up into the saddle with ease.

"Where did a girl like you learn to ride a horse?" Zhihao asked her.

"In my dreams," she said with a smile.

With half of the day used up, but not totally wasted, the little exploring party set off on the road to Jehol.

EIGHT

*J*iayi was thrilled with her new clothes. She had never had such freedom of movement, at least not in this life. She was reminded of how Lady Meirong must have felt during the Tang Dynasty. She could walk normally, ride a horse, and soon she would be climbing rocks and exploring caves, all things she never could have done in her old clothes.

They had lost half a day finding her new clothes, so they had to move quickly for the rest of the day. It would take them two or three days to reach the Conghua Pass, halfway to Jehol.

Zhihao was riding in the front, leading their small expedition. Jiayi was in the middle, and she was followed by Eunuch Lo, with the mule taking up the rear.

The small group finally reached their first campsite much later than they planned. It was nearly dark. Eunuch Lo worked quickly to build the tents while Zhihao worked out a plan for the next day. They were traveling too slowly and the terrain had changed over the decades. Zhihao needed to compare maps and come up with a plan for the next day while they still had light.

Jiayi took off her gloves and wandered the area collecting firewood. The gloves made her hands sweaty and she was already getting blisters from the reigns. There were sparse trees. The area was arid and rocky. While Eunuch Lo was clearly annoyed at getting dusty as he worked around the camp, Jiayi was excited to be climbing around the rocks in her new boots.

"Do not wander too far, Jiayi," Zhihao called out to her as she slipped behind a large boulder.

"I won't," she called back. So far, she was only finding small dry sticks, nothing that would help them build a substantial fire. As she wandered, she eventually came to a small outcropping. It wasn't exactly a cave because it wasn't very deep—she could see all the way to the back from the entrance. She could tell it had been used as a shelter because there was a pile of firewood in it, an old fire pit, and some abandoned items.

Jiayi used a stick to rifle around the items. She was careful to not touch old items she wasn't familiar with. She never knew just how old they could be and whether they would send her into a trance. Jiayi did not find much, only some old rags and torn papers with faded writing.

The sun was near setting, and the last of the sun's rays were shining directly into the cave. Jiayi moved deeper into the cave to see if she could find anything else of use. She kicked at the pebbles on the ground and found a small coin. She bent to pick it up without thinking and promptly passed out.

"I'll never betray the emperor!" she was shouting as she awoke.

A man dressed in court robes grabbed her arm. "You will do as you are told or else!" he yelled in her face.

"Or else what?" she asked. Jiayi had no idea what was going on or who she was, but something felt familiar, so she just let the woman whose body she was inhabiting remain in control.

"Have I not made that perfectly clear, you stupid bitch?" the man spat. "You will help us or else your whole family will suffer! Your parents, your brothers. They will all die, but not before they see you executed, slice by slice."

He was talking about the Death by a Thousand Cuts. A horrid and barbaric way to die. It was so disgusting, Jiayi's empress had recently outlawed the practice. But wherever she was now, it was clearly still in use. It was a death usually reserved for the most severe of crimes—treason.

"No!" she cried. "Please, please not my family! But what you ask of me, it is impossible! I'm just a bedmate for the emperor. Nothing more. How can I get you what you want?"

The man ran his finger down the side of her face. "Lady Cai, do not play coy. We all know you are far more than that. The emperor is infatuated with you. He trusts you. Do I dare say he loves you? Is he such a fool as to love a woman? A whore such as you?"

Jiayi shook her head to get away from the man's odious touch. So, she was once again Lady Cai. But what was she doing here? And who was this man?

"I am not a whore," she growled. "I am the consort to the emperor. The mother of his child. You are nothing, Minister Shun. If the emperor finds out what you are up to, it is you who will die by a thousand cuts!"

The man smirked. "Not a whore?" He pulled a single coin out of his pocket and flipped it at her. She caught it in her hand and looked at it. It was the same coin she had picked up from the floor of the cave. "You have already taken far more than that from me to help support your family in exchange for your compliance. Finish the job. Get me something, *anything* I can use to overthrow the emperor, and you will be rewarded with more gold than you can possibly imagine..."

Jiayi looked back down at the coin in her hand as the world faded to black.

She opened her eyes and the world was dark. How long was she out? She sat up and realized that she was still in the outcropping, but the sun had set. Zhihao and Eunuch Lo must be worried about her. She put the coin in her pocket and grabbed the bits of leftover firewood as she ran out of the cave.

She made it back to camp as Zhihao was giving an earful to Eunuch Lo.

"She could be anywhere! She could have been eaten by wolves or kidnapped! How could you let her out of your sight?" he yelled.

"Kidnapped by wolves?" she asked with a smile on her face as she approached them, trying to diffuse the situation.

"Jiayi!" Zhihao said, running to her. "Are you all right? Were you hurt?"

"I'm just fine," she said, handing him her bundle of wood.

"Where were you?" Zhihao asked as he tossed the sticks aside.

"I was looking for wood, like you told me to do, and I found something." She fished into her pocket and handed him the coin.

"A coin?" he asked, taking the coin and examining it closely. "A bit old. From the...Daoguang era!"

"How can you tell?" she asked.

"Every emperor mints his own coins. See the character here at the top? That means it was made during the reign of the Daoguang Emperor."

Jiayi looked at the coin and nodded, as if she knew what the character he was pointing to meant. It meant nothing to her, but she couldn't let him know that.

"But what does it mean?" Zhihao asked. "If anything? You can buy buckets of old coins in the market, and random coins can be found everywhere. And this is a common road. Anyone could have dropped it."

"But not just anyone did," Jiayi said with a proud smile.

"What did you see, Jiayi?" Zhihao asked.

"Who was Minister Shun?" she replied.

"He was Emperor Daoguang's highest ranking minister," Zhihao explained. "They didn't get along, but Minister Shun served Daoguang's father, the Jiaqing Emperor, and served Daoguang for most of his reign."

"Did Shun ever attempt any sort of coup that you know of?" Jiayi asked.

"There isn't any on record," Zhihao said. "Why? What do you know?"

"I think this Minister Shun tried to use Lady Cai against the emperor," she said. "And he paid her with this coin. I found it in a cave, an outcropping of stone. Lady Cai and Minister Shun met in that cave and he told her that if she did not do as he said and help him overthrow the emperor, he would kill her and her entire family."

"I can't believe what you are saying," Zhihao said. "Minister Shun was an important man. He served two emperors during a very difficult time. Lady Cai was a disgraced consort. She was only honored after her death because her son was honored by the next emperor. This is...this is shocking and completely contradicts what we know about history."

"Maybe history is wrong," Jiayi said.

"What do you mean?" Zhihao asked.

"I mean, what we think we know, what people have written, it could all be wrong. Lies meant to protect some people and discredit others," she said.

"History is written by the victors, as they say," Zhihao replied.

"What did you mean when you said Lady Cai was disgraced?" Jiayi asked.

"Lady Cai was demoted not long after the events we have been investigating," he explained. "I don't know why. There aren't many records about the management of the Inner Court."

"Maybe the emperor found out about her role in the attempted coup," Jiayi said. "But he took pity on her because of their love or because she was protecting her family, so he just demoted her instead of having her put to death."

"It's possible," Zhihao said. "But we have no way of really knowing."

"True," Jiayi said. "But at least we have a new lead on the seal."

"We do?" Zhihao asked.

"What if the seal wasn't lost," Jiayi said. "What if she gave it to Minister Shun."

NINE

*T*hat night, Zhihao crept out of his tent. When he arrived at Jiayi's tent, Eunuch Lo was still awake, guarding the entrance.

"I need to speak to Jiayi," Zhihao whispered. "I need to talk to her more about her visions. I have some more theories."

Eunuch Lo nodded and let Zhihao enter, but he left the tent flap open a crack so he could keep an ever-watchful eye on them.

Jiayi was sitting on the blankets she was going to sleep under later. On her lap was a stack of papers and she was holding a charcoal pencil in her hand. Her face blushed when she saw him and quickly moved to hide what she was working on. She was wearing a long thick robe—even in summer the nights would get chilly north of Peking—but she clutched it closed at the neck upon seeing him, gray streaks of charcoal staining the fabric in the process.

"You shouldn't be here," she said as she clumsily tried to stack her pages into a folio with one hand.

"Eunuch Lo is watching us," he said.

Jiayi pressed her lips and then nodded. "He always is," she whispered as she pushed her folio aside. "He guards me at the palace as well."

Zhihao wasn't sure what to think of that or why she was telling him such a thing. It was odd that the empress felt the need to guard the girl, as if she might run away or be stolen. Jiayi had told him she was like a kept pet. Maybe she felt like a prisoner.

"Are you sketching something new?" he asked, remembering that she said she sketched the things she saw. "Something you have seen? Can I see them?"

She shook her head. "It's nothing that would be of any use."

He doubted that and figured she was just being modest, but he accepted her excuse for now. "I was just wondering if there was anything else from your vision you learned," he said, folding up a blanket to sit on across from her.

"I think I told you everything," she said. "Are you documenting what I have told you? The things about history that might not be correct?"

Even though he had already stated to Jiayi why he was there, she naturally spoke around the topic at hand, making polite conversation first. Zhihao often found this sort of tradition annoying—he was a busy man who liked to speak plainly—but he found that he enjoyed his conversations with Jiayi, so he did not push her to tell him more about her visions until she was ready.

"I have been," he said. "But I am not sure what I will do with the information. I don't have any concrete evidence to back up my claims. This isn't like any of the digs I went on in Egypt."

"What is a 'dig?'" she asked. "And what is Egypt?"

"Oh, sorry. I mean an archeological dig, where we look

for old artifacts and cities buried under the ground. Egypt is a country in Northern Africa. That is where there are pharaohs and pyramids. Lots of exciting things are being unearthed every day. The excavation model being followed in Egypt is something China should look to. Our thousands of years of history should not be lost."

Jiayi smiled as though she was uncomfortable. "Forgive me. I must be terribly stupid. I only understood half of what you were talking about."

"Not at all," he said. "You should forgive me. I am used to speaking to men and women who are in the same field as I am and understand the lingo."

"There are women in your field?" she asked. "Women...archeologists?"

"Sort of," he said. "Few women go to university, and even fewer are willing to battle the elements of the desert or attempt to survive in an alien culture. But some brilliant women are linguists...err, people who study language, or women who try to fix old paintings or sculptures. Those sorts of jobs seem naturally suited to women."

"I would be willing to learn such things," Jiayi said. "I want to learn many things. I feel like my mind is empty and begging to be filled. I have already learned so much from you."

"We can hope that the end of our expedition will not be the end of our—" He wanted to say friendship, but that would have been too personal. "Of our...adventures together."

Jiayi nodded. "I do hope," she said. "My visions are like dreams. Have you ever had a dream so real, so vivid, that you thought you were living in it? And when you awoke, you thought you would never forget it? But later, when you try to tell someone about your dream, you cannot hardly recall it at all?"

Zhihao nodded.

"My visions are like that," she said. "If I do not relay them immediately, I forget."

"You should try writing them down," Zhihao said. "Not only so you can use the details to find artifacts, but just because they are interesting. And what if there are links between your visions? Or patterns that could help you deduce when or where you might travel to next. They would be fascinating to analyze."

"I do suppose you are right," she said with a tight smile and then looked back at the lantern instead of having to make eye contact with him.

"Do you remember anything else from your vision earlier?" he asked.

"I don't know," she said. "I just remember that Minister Shun was very intimidating. He was frightening. He threatened Lady Cai with the Death by a Thousand Cuts."

"Well, she wasn't put to death, we know that," Zhihao said. "So we know his threats came to nothing."

"Oh, I wanted to ask," Jiayi said. "You are sure you don't know anything about Lady Cai being disgraced?"

"Records from the Inner Court, the court of the women, are sparse," he said. "I suppose historians and scholars don't think the lives of women are important enough to include in official records."

Jiayi scoffed, and Zhihao laughed a little.

"I didn't say I agree with it, just stating their viewpoint," he clarified. "After all, women exert a lot of influence over their husbands and often run the household while the men are doing other things. It would be interesting to know just how the women of the Inner Court have influenced government policy throughout history."

"I don't think many men could handle the shock," Jiayi said with a smirk.

"Perhaps not," he agreed. "Your vision today was probably before the seal was lost," he said, changing the subject. "Minister Shun could have threatened Lady Cai here, after their first day on the road, telling her she needed to find something to use against the emperor. Two days later, they are attacked at the Conghua Pass. The emperor gives Lady Cai the seal. Lady Cai realizes that Minister Shun could use it against the emperor and gives it to him."

"Or she *didn't* give it to the minister," Jiayi said. "There is no record of a coup, and she wasn't executed for treason. Maybe she hid it or gave it to someone she could trust."

"Perhaps," Zhihao said. "But if that was the case, why not retrieve the seal later?"

"When we find the seal, I am sure we will find out," she replied.

Zhihao laughed. "Indeed. *When*, not *if*."

TEN

The next morning, as Zhihao and Jiayi were eating bowls of congee by the fire, Eunuch Lo approached and motioned for Zhihao to follow him. Zhihao did so, and Jiayi followed as well. He led them a few feet from the fire and pointed at the ground. There were boot prints and a small scattering of spent cigarettes.

"Someone was in the camp last night," Zhihao said. "And it looks like he was watching us for a while. Did you see anyone last night?"

Eunuch Lo only shook his head.

"We must be more careful, then," Zhihao said. "Don't leave anything unattended. Make sure the horses are secure. And someone should be on watch at all times during the night. Eunuch Lo and I will have to take shifts."

"Who do you think it could be?" Jiayi asked.

"No idea," Zhihao said. "Could be anyone. I'm sure there are other travelers or bandits hanging about."

"Bandits?" asked Jiayi, alarmed.

"I'm sure we will be fine," Zhihao said with a smile. "Nothing to worry about. Come on, let's get moving."

The small party once again mounted their horses. They were still moving very slowly. The quality of the road was poor—uneven ruts, holes, and mud puddles prevented them from gaining any real speed.

"I didn't expect the road to be so bad," Zhihao commented. "I would think a road used for imperial processions would be well-worn."

"It hasn't been used for imperial processions in decades," Jiayi said. "The empress hates Jehol. She hasn't been there since the death of her husband. She prefers the Summer Palace at Yuan Ming Yuan, to the west."

"Yes, we are all aware of her fondness for Yuan Ming Yuan," Zhihao quipped.

The British had destroyed Yuan Ming Yuan when they occupied Peking over forty years ago. The empress had spent the rest of her life—and an untold amount of money —attempting to rebuild it. Yuan Ming Yuan was a sore point for people dissatisfied with Manchu rule.

"The empress doesn't go on extended hunting trips like the emperors who ruled before her," Jiayi said. "She doesn't take official visits around the country or to other lands like some kings and emperors do. She stays home and rules China day in and day out, and she is nearly seventy years old! She should be enjoying her graying years. Yet she is still up before dawn every day, working for her country. Should she not have a place of rest?"

Zhihao laughed. "For someone who considers herself the empress's pet, you are sure defensive of her," he said. "Perhaps some time away from her has altered your perception."

Jiayi blushed, but she supposed he was right. She did feel different, and she had only left the Forbidden City barely a day before. She felt stronger, energized. She felt free to speak her mind. Was it the fresh air? The new clothes? Being in the company of a man who valued what she had to say and listened to her? She wasn't sure. But she knew her life would not be the same after this trip. Would she be able to go back to the Forbidden City? Back to her caged little world? She was almost certain she would not. But what would she be able to do about it? The empress would not let her go. And if she could get away from the empress, where would she go? How would she take care of herself? If only she knew how much her stash of pilfered items was worth and how to sell it. Jiayi sighed to herself and thought of the items she had hidden in her bag. She was afraid to leave them behind in case someone snooped around her room while she was gone. It was dangerous to be traveling with them, but what else could she do? But those were all problems for another day. For now, she needed to enjoy this little excursion.

Finally, they came to a small town that was surrounded by a brick wall. They presented their travel documents from the capital that stated they were scholars on a research trip and had no problem gaining entrance to the town. The town had several homes, a few businesses, and one inn. They rented two rooms for the night—one for Zhihao and one for Jiayi and Eunuch Lo. They also purchased hot baths for each of them.

That evening, while Eunuch Lo was resting in their room while Jiayi and Zhihao were eating bowls of noodles in the dining hall, another group of men arrived—Chinese men and foreigners. Although their clothes were filthy, Jiayi could see they were dressed similarly to Zhihao. They loudly ordered baths and bowls of food. They were overly friendly to the women who were serving food—even touching them—and their voices boomed. They made Jiayi nervous. She looked at her bowl, hoping they would go away, and Zhihao nervously tapped his fingers on the table.

"Who are they?" Jiayi whispered.

"British treasure hunters," Zhihao said.

"And those Chinese men?" she asked.

"Men who went to school in England as well," Zhihao said, irritated.

"You mean they were your classmates?" Jiayi asked.

"No," Zhihao explained. "They were a few years older than me."

Just then, the men saw them. They walked over and said something to the group, but it was in English. Jiayi didn't understand everything they said, though, to her surprise, she had a general idea.

One of the white men sat down next to Jiayi and tried to put his arm around her.

"I didn't expect to see someone so pretty way out here," he said in English.

Jiayi understood what he said, but she didn't know how to respond, so she just said, "Hello," while not taking her eyes off her bowl.

The men laughed. Then the one sitting next to her said, in Chinese, "Very good! Though you could learn a lot more English from a natural speaker, don't you think?"

Jiayi couldn't help but look at him in surprise. "You speak Chinese?" she asked in Chinese.

He laughed again. "Of course. You cannot spend years among heathens without learning some of their ways." He and his whole party laughed as though he had just made a great joke.

"Leave my...sister alone, Marcus," Zhihao said, in Chinese.

"Oh, your sister. My mistake, Mister High and Mighty,"

Marcus replied to Zhihao. Marcus then leaned over to Jiayi and said, "You wouldn't believe how uptight this guy is. I think he has a pole shoved straight up his arse."

Jiayi pursed her lips to keep from smiling, but Marcus must have sensed her strain.

"I guess you would know better than I, Little Miss Teddy, having to live with the poor bastard."

"Teddy?" Jiayi asked, thinking it was some sort of slang term.

"His English name," Marcus said. "He called himself Theodore, but everyone else called him Teddy."

"Not everyone," Zhihao said through gritted teeth. "Just inconsiderate boors like you."

"Ted-dy," Jiayi repeated slowly, causing the men to laugh.

"She's got it!" Marcus said, slapping his hand on the table to another round of laughter.

Jiayi knew she should be cautious around such men, but she found their happiness infectious. She wished she could be so carefree.

"What are you doing out here?" Zhihao asked.

"What we always do, Teddy," Marcus said. "Looking for gold." At that, he reached into his pocket and plunked a worn gold artifact on the table. It was small, but looked carved.

"Where did you find that?" Zhihao asked.

"There's a wee cave a ways back," Marcus said. "Not much there, but we found a few trinkets. It's along the path to the old Mountain Palace. But if we did a more substantial dig, we could find more."

"I found a coin there," Jiayi said.

"Look at you!" Marcus said, squeezing her arms. "You're a little archeologist in the making, aren't you?"

Jiayi blushed, but she didn't push him away.

"Here," he said, offering her the little hunk of gold. "Take a closer look."

Jiayi shook her head, afraid of what would happen if she touched it. She had taken off her gloves before eating. "I couldn't."

"It won't bite," he said. "But look here." He held the artifact up and pointed at it. "See how it is narrow at the top and then gets wide here in the middle. I think this might be an old fertility statue. See, these little indentations are the face, and these are her hands, then ample breasts and thighs."

Jiayi was a little worried he was teasing her again, trying to make her uncomfortable by speaking of such things, but once he pointed them out, she was able to see the statue's features. She was amazed by what he was able to discern from the figure with his trained eye. She looked at Marcus, trying to see if he was lying or joking, but his interest in the statue seemed genuine.

"That's fascinating," she finally said.

"It is!" he said. "Glad you appreciate such things. I can get a lot of money for something like this back in England."

"You are going to sell it?" Jiayi asked, using a napkin to wipe her mouth.

"Of course he is," Zhihao snapped. "He's not an archeologist. He's a treasure hunter. He just pilfers tombs for things he can sell."

"Make a good living at it. The English are mad for Chinese *kitsch*," he said.

"What is *kitsch*?" Jiayi asked.

"Oh, bits and bobbles. Anything Oriental. Statues, vases, porcelain, jewelry, paintings, embroidery. Anything exotic people can display in their homes."

"And you dig up this...*kitsch* and then sell it in England?" she asked.

"Not always. Sometimes I just buy it from people for a low price and mark it up a hundred times when I get it to England. People have no idea what their old junk is worth."

"Heirlooms," Zhihao corrected. "You steal people's heirlooms, their family history, and mark it up for your own gain."

"Hey, I don't steal anything. Everything I have, I bought fair and square or dug out of the ground myself."

"Out of Chinese ground," Zhihao spat. "The Chinese government didn't give you permission to collect and sell our history. Those items should stay in China."

"The Chinese aren't doing anything to protect them. Without us, this stuff would just be lost to time. At least this way the stuff could end up in museums or proper households."

"And will you burn the houses and temples when you are done raiding them, like your country did to Yuan Ming Yuan?"

"Hey, that was a long time ago, Teddy—"

"I remember. We all remember."

The mood of the room had darkened. Marcus and Zhihao stared at each other, not saying a word. Jiayi wanted to know more about selling the artifacts. She wondered if Marcus would be interested in buying the items she had stashed away, but she couldn't mention them here, in front of Zhihao. She did have one question, though.

"Egypt," she said. The men all looked at her as if she had just spoken French. "Egypt," she said again. "Zhihao, you said you went on a dig to Egypt."

"Yes?" he said, confused.

"Did you have permission from the Egyptian govern-ment to dig for items? What happened to the things that you dug up?"

"Oh-ho-ho," said Marcus. "Such a clever little lass! Yes, *Zhihao*, what did happen to the things you dug up in Egypt?"

"That...that was different..." he stammered. "I was just a student. That was still *British* interference."

"You're never wrong, are you, Teddy?" Marcus asked, but he didn't bother waiting for an answer. "So, where is your little party headed?" Marcus asked.

"Nowhere particular," Zhihao said.

"I see," Marcus said, elbowing Jiayi. "Secret mission? Hot tip on a big stash? I understand. Have to keep quiet."

Jiayi looked away, not wanting her face to confirm what he was saying.

"Well, good luck to you, old friends...and new ones," Marcus said. He took Jiayi's hand and kissed the back of it. She felt her cheeks heat again and quickly pulled her hand away. She could almost feel Zhihao glaring at her.

Marcus and his group then tromped to the back of the building where the bathhouse was. Jiayi returned to her now cold noodles, avoiding Zhihao's gaze.

"You shouldn't have encouraged him," he finally said.

"I don't know what you are talking about," she mumbled. "But do you think he or his men were the ones in our camp? He said he was in the same area. And someone had been camping in the cave where I found the coin."

"Not sure what reason he would have for being in our camp," Zhihao said. "But it is possible. Be sure to lock your door tonight."

Jiayi clenched her teeth to keep from arguing. She was,

of course, going to lock her door. She also had Eunuch Lo with her, and he would not let anyone enter. While she did not hope that Marcus would try to sneak into her room that night, she did hope to see him again. As she palmed the gold statue, safely wrapped in her napkin, she had a feeling Marcus would be able to help her escape.

ELEVEN

Zhihao tossed and turned all night in a huff. He couldn't believe the way Marcus was so friendly to Jiayi. And she did nothing to discourage him! In fact, she was encouraging him with the way she smiled demurely and asked questions and made reasonable arguments... How dare she! Well, once they found that stupid seal and this insane quest was at an end, he'd leave her to rot in that stuffy palace. He'd never have to see her again.

What was Marcus really doing out here anyway? He knew that Marcus had already made a lot of money selling artifacts he had dug up the previous year in Chang'an, one of China's historical capital cities. Why would he be here, in the middle of nowhere collecting cheap trinkets off the ground? As he admitted, he could make more money in Peking buying family heirlooms and never once having to use a shovel. It didn't make sense. He must have had a lead on something important in the area. He couldn't know about the seal, could he?

It seemed like a lot of people knew about the seal. If the empress knew, she must have learned about it from her husband, the Xianfeng Emperor. But the emperor had other wives and concubines. The Daoguang Emperor's other women could have known as well, and possibly his top magistrates. Had Prince Gong known? How many men in the know had women who knew also? How many people had those gossips told over the years? Somehow, Hu Xiaosheng knew. The legend of the lost seal had traveled so far and wide, it would be impossible to know who knew what and when. If more people knew about the lost seal than Zhihao first realized, how many people also knew more to the story? Knew about the ambush? Knew about Lady Cai? What if Zhihao wasn't the only person looking for the seal?

By morning, Zhihao was anxious to get started. Any wasted moment could mean someone else getting closer to finding the seal. As the party gathered at their horses, everyone looked refreshed and ready to go. A warm bath, a hearty meal, and a good sleep had reenergized them. Only Zhihao seemed to be out of sorts. Even though he had fumed over Jiayi and Marcus all night, as soon as he saw her in her silly outfit, he couldn't help but smile.

"Did you not sleep well, Zhihao?" she asked kindly.

"No," he admitted. "I am ready to get going. We need to find the seal. I have a feeling we are not the only ones looking for it."

"Do you think Marcus is looking for it?" Jiayi asked, her voice low even though no one else was around.

Zhihao nodded. "I do. Or he could be looking for something else and come across it. I just have a bad feeling."

The group headed toward the pass. The roads were drier today, so they made better time. They finally arrived at the Conghua Pass in the early evening when there was still light. As they rounded a corner and the pass spread out before them, Jiayi gasped.

"I...I've been here before," she said. "This is where the battle was."

"What can you tell us?" Zhihao asked.

She pointed to a wide open area with a stream running through it. "There were many tents set up here for people who were traveling with the imperial family. The attackers charged through the tents, waving their weapons and killing people as they tried to escape."

She got down off her horse and walked around the area, looking for something. "There was a trail..." She looked around. "There, to the west, that led from the lower camp up here to the level we are at. Up here is where the emperor's tent was. The generals could watch the battle below and better protect the emperor from here."

"That makes sense," Zhihao said. "The higher vantage point would be easier to defend. We should set up our own camp here."

After they finished setting up the tents and building a fire, the group was at a bit of a loss as to what to do.

"So, what now?" Jiayi asked. "If this is where the tent was, if this is where the emperor gave the seal to Lady Cai, what do we do now?"

"Let's survey the area," Zhihao said. "Look for abandoned paths, caves, any markers. Anything that looks unnatural or manmade."

Zhihao and Jiayi each grabbed a water canteen and Zhihao took a small haversack with maps and binoculars. Eunuch Lo stayed to keep an eye on the camp. As soon as they crested a small hill where they had a good view of the area, Zhihao opened his pack and pulled out a piece of red silk.

"Jiayi, can you touch this and tell me if you see anything?"

"What is it?" she asked.

"It is the silk lining from the box that contained the seal. The empress wouldn't let me bring the whole box, but since this also touched the seal, I thought it might work to spur your visions."

"I suppose," she said as she removed one of her gloves. "But I can't promise I will see anything from the time period we need."

"I know," he said. "But we have to try. We don't have anything else to go on right now."

Jiayi nodded her head and found a flat rock to sit on. "Will you keep me from falling over?" she asked.

Zhihao nodded and sat next to her, putting his hands on her shoulders. She took a deep breath as she reached for the silk. She lost consciousness almost instantly, going limp. Zhihao leaned her against the tree and then stood to take in his surroundings. The area was dry and rocky. There were not many trees, and the trees he could see looked as brown as the dusty ground. One rock looked pretty much like the next. He wasn't sure if they would be able to find anything out here. But Jiayi had recognized the area where the battle and camp were. Maybe she would be able to recognize more of the area from her vision.

He pulled out his binoculars to survey the area. On his map, he began to mark areas that were probably cave openings. He was lost in thought, enjoying his work, so he did not hear the footsteps approach until it was too late.

"Well, what do we have here?" a gruff voice asked from behind him.

"Are you having a little private time with that pretty girl?" another asked.

Zhihao turned and saw two men he didn't recognize. They were dressed rough and their hair was a mess. They both held large knives. "Who are you?" he asked. "What do you want?"

"Any money or valuables you have on you, for start," the first man said.

"And that little sweet thing for seconds," the second man said, motioning to Jiayi as he deftly bounced his knife from one hand to the other.

"Don't be ridiculous," Zhihao said. "I don't have anything on me. It's all back at my camp."

"Guess we will just take the girl then," one of the men said.

"Like hell you will," Zhihao said, putting up his fists. He wasn't sure how he was going to stop them. He didn't have a weapon, and while he was a fairly good boxer, these men were bigger than him and had knives they undoubtedly knew how to use.

"Hey, what's wrong with her?" one of the men asked, motioning to Jiayi, who was still deep in her trance against the tree. "She drugged or something?"

Zhihao had no idea if he could wake her up or how long she would be out. She had taken a deep breath, most likely planning on being gone for as long as possible, so she could be asleep for five or six minutes or more.

"Mind your own business and move along," Zhihao said, holding up his fists.

The two men laughed, then one of them lunged toward him. Zhihao jumped aside, but then the other man grabbed one of his arms. He tried to wrench free, but then the first man came back and punched him in the gut. Zhihao gasped as the wind flew out of him. The man then brandished his knife.

"I'm gonna enjoy this," the bandit said. "Then, I'm gonna enjoy your little woman."

Zhihao gritted his teeth and was about to attempt to break free when the man grunted and turned around. Eunuch Lo was standing behind him, his face hard as granite. He had punched the man in his kidney. As the man turned, Eunuch Lo punched him twice in the stomach and then once in the face, causing the man to fall unconscious.

The other man let go of one of Zhihao's arms just long enough to grab his knife and hold it to Zhihao's throat.

"I don't know where you keep your balls, but you got some big ones," the man said. "But try anything else and your friend here gets it."

Eunuch Lo stood still. Zhihao's eyes were darting around as he was trying to formulate a plan when he heard a *thunk*. His captor went rigid, then he dropped his knife and fell over. Zhihao turned around and saw Jiayi holding a large rock.

"It's a good thing I am used to waking up in weird situations," she said.

Zhihao smiled. She certainly was quick on her feet. Zhihao and Eunuch Lo worked together to tie the bandits up.

"What are we going to do with them?" Jiayi asked. "We can't guard them all the time or take them with us."

"We should question them at least," Zhihao said. "What if someone sent them to kill us?"

"Who would do that?" Jiayi asked. "Who even knows we are out here?"

"Marcus," Zhihao said.

"You don't really think that, do you?" Jiayi asked.

Zhihao snorted. Did she really think Marcus was innocent? Blameless? She was smitten with the man!

"Who else could it be?" Zhihao asked, more harshly than he planned.

"It doesn't matter," Jiayi said. "It is nearly dark. We need to do something."

Jiayi and Zhihao were still arguing with each other when they heard a sound like a muffled punch followed by a grunt. They turned and saw Eunuch Lo removing a large knife from the gut of one of the men. The other man was looking around wildly and crying for help through his stifling mouth gag.

"Eunuch Lo!" Zhihao cried out. "What are you doing?"

"What you lack the courage to do," he said calmly as he moved behind the other man and seamlessly slit his throat.

Jiayi and Zhihao watched in horror as blood spilled from the two men and pooled around them. Zhihao protectively put his arm around Jiayi.

"How...how could you?" Jiayi finally managed to ask.

"I am here to protect you," Eunuch Lo said as he wiped the blood from the blade and then slipped it into his waistband. "I will do that by any means necessary." He then walked over and grabbed one of the shovels they had brought with them. "You should go back to the camp and rest," he said. "It is dark. We can continue looking for the seal tomorrow."

Zhihao and Jiayi turned and quickly walked back toward the camp. When they thought they were finally out of earshot, Zhihao spoke first.

"We cannot stay here," he said.

"What else can we do?" Jiayi asked. "We have to keep looking for the seal. We can't just leave."

"We cannot stay here with him. He's a murderer!"

"I don't think we have a choice," Jiayi said.

"What?" Zhihao asked. "How can you not be terrified of that man?"

"Who says I'm not?" she asked. "But what choice do we have? The empress has ordered us to find the seal, and I fear her more than Eunuch Lo."

"But what if we are on the completely wrong track?" Zhihao asked. "What if we don't find it and Eunuch Lo has orders to take care of us next?"

"And you think running is the answer?" Jiayi asked. "If we return to the empress without the seal, what do you think she will do to us then?"

Zhihao paced in circles. "We are so dead!"

"Not if we find the seal," Jiayi said.

Zhihao shook his head. "Fine, fine. We will stay here. Are you all right?"

"No," she said honestly. "I'm terrified. I had no idea he was capable of such a thing. He'll be right outside my tent..." She shook her head as her voice trailed off.

Zhihao nodded. "I know," he said. "I'm sorry. I wish there was something I could do."

"We just need to find the seal and bring this journey to an end," she said.

"Oh, by the way," Zhihao said. "What did you see earlier?"

"Not much. Lady Cai did take the seal, wrapped in the cloth. By then, the battle had ended. She then went to a smaller tent and wrote a letter. That was all I saw before I woke up and saw the men attacking you."

"That was quick thinking, with the rock," Zhihao said, rubbing the back of his head.

"Thanks," she replied with a smile.

"What did the letter say?" he asked.

"I...I don't know," she stammered as if embarrassed,

though Zhihao couldn't tell of what. "In the dreams, words are always...muddled, backward. Like looking at them through water. Though I can usually hear the thoughts of the person reading or writing, they never think exactly what they are writing. I'm sorry. I can't remember what the letter was about, but...it...umm...oh! It was to her brother, her younger brother."

"Maybe she was writing to her brother for help or advice," Zhihao said. "But surely he is long dead by now."

"Let's just hope she didn't send the seal to him," Jiayi said. "It could be anywhere in China!"

"Indeed," Zhihao said. Just then, he spied Eunuch Lo heading toward them. "We better retire for the night. If you need anything, just scream. I'll hear you."

"That is far more comforting than it should be," Jiayi said.

TWELVE

*J*iayi could hardly sleep a wink. She had never cared for Eunuch Lo. She resenting being monitored like a naughty child and worried about the power he held over her after he saw her steal the empress's comb. But she had never feared him as she did now. He was always watching her, staring at her, always nearby, which made her uncomfortable, but he was under orders from the empress to keep an eye on her, and she was valuable to the empress. She never thought he would harm her. But now, she wasn't so sure.

Seeing those two men murdered in cold blood in front of her had upset her more than she realized at the time. As the night wore on, the shock wore off and the gravity of the situation sank in. Every time she closed her eyes, she saw the terrified face of the second man and felt his fear. She felt as though she should have done...something, but she had no idea what. Logically, she knew there was nothing she could have done in the moment. It had never entered into her mind that the men's lives could be in danger. But she felt guilty nonetheless. And afraid. She wanted to be comforted. She longed for the arms of a man around her. Prince Junjie's arms. But she could not go to him now. Not because she was worried about draining her powers, but because she had already tried and found she could not. Her vision with the silk had drained her, and even now, hours later, as she palmed Lady Meirong's necklace in her hand, nothing happened.

She had gotten nothing from the silk that would help them. She couldn't believe the majority of her vision had been wasted on Lady Cai writing a letter. At least Zhihao seemed to believe her about why she had been unable to read it.

She also couldn't sleep because she couldn't get her idea of running away with Marcus out of her head. She didn't find him particularly handsome, and she didn't trust him, but the prospect of asking him to help her escape to a foreign country thrilled her to the core. She had dreamed of running away from the Forbidden City and the empress for years, but this was the first time she had met someone who could, theoretically, help her get away.

She had no idea if she would see him again, or if he would be willing to help her, but she had to work up her courage to ask him for help if she saw him. She wasn't sure why Zhihao disliked him so. Probably some professional rivalry. He couldn't be as bad of a man as he let on. He spoke Chinese! That wasn't easy. He had to have some affection for her country. Perhaps he would have sympathy for her plight.

Unable to sleep, she sketched. She opened her notebook and used her coal pencil to continue working on an image she had started several days before. It was of the Conghua Pass. She wasn't sure why she felt compelled to draw a landscape. She wasn't very good at it and much preferred to draw the faces of the people she had met in her visions. She had more than a few sketches of Prince Junjie. Yet when she felt the urge to create something, she could not rest until she finished it. She loved the feeling of the charcoal as it ran slightly rough over the thick paper. Her fingers turned black as she smoothed out lines and filled in shadows. By the light of her lantern, the hours ticked by. It was probably near dawn by the time she laid her pencil down and her mind had calmed enough for her to get a little rest.

She rose with the sun and dressed quickly, trying to keep the many thoughts that still whirled in her head at bay. She avoided looking at Eunuch Lo as she exited the tent. He seemed to sense her unease and went to the edge of the camp, keeping an eye out on every desert rodent that scurried past or leaf that drifted by. She then prepared the morning congee. The air was cool and crisp up here in this place even though it was summer, and the sun rising over the hills was a rainbow of colors. During the dry, hot parts of the day, it was hard to imagine that such a place could also be so beautiful and peaceful. She dreamed of one day learning to paint with watercolors or oils so she could bring such colorful scenes to life, but even asking the empress for paper and charcoal sometimes felt like asking the empress for bars of gold. The empress was a stingy woman. Every coin she could save from her household expenses she spent on her summer palace. And that meant every thread of silk, every pot of face paint, and every stick of charcoal had to be used sparingly.

Jiayi sighed as she looked out over rocks as far as the eye could see, some rising, some dipping. She had no idea where in this endless sea of stones the seal could be, if it was here at all.

Zhihao finally emerged from his tent looking as though

he had had a rough night as well. He stumbled over to the fire and boiled some water. Surprisingly, he didn't use it to fix tea, but some strong-smelling brown stuff.

"Coffee," Zhihao explained, letting her take a sip. She couldn't help making a face. He laughed. "Something I started drinking when I was in England. It's an acquired taste, but it will help you wake up when you are tired."

"I'm sorry you didn't sleep well," Jiayi said.

"Every noise made me jump," Zhihao said. He eyed Eunuch Lo across the camp and kept his voice low. "I was worried someone was in the camp or something might happen and I wouldn't hear it. But I was also trying to figure out where to search today. From looking at the maps, I think there are several caves in the area, mostly to the west. We should probably head that way."

Jiayi had no reason to agree or disagree with his plan, so as soon as they had eaten, the group headed out with shovels, ropes, pickaxes, and other items. They had only walked a short distance when they saw a man with a herd of goats. The man was probably not as old as he looked, but years of sun and wind had weathered his face. His clothing was worn but brightly colored, indicating that he belonged to a specific ethnic minority that lived in the area.

"Maybe we should ask him if he knows anything that could help us," Jiayi suggested.

Zhihao nodded in agreement. "Hello, sir!" he called out with a smile as they approached. "We are looking for a good place to dig for lost historical items. Can you tell us anything about the area?" he asked in his Peking dialect.

The man replied, but it was clear Zhihao could not understand him. The man spoke a northern dialect that was nothing like Peking Chinese.

"I guess we won't get anything out of this fellow," Zhihao said. "I can't communicate with him."

"He says he can't understand you," Jiayi said with a chuckle.

"You...you understand him?" Zhihao asked.

"A little bit," Jiayi said.

"Can you speak to him?" Zhihao asked.

"Possibly," she said. "I have heard his dialect before, but I've never spoken it...when I was awake."

"You can remember the languages you have heard and spoken in your visions?" he asked, astonished. "Is that how you knew what Marcus was saying to you in English? I thought you were just guessing by his body language. Can you speak English?"

"It's...complicated," she said. "I'll explain later. We don't want to keep this kind fellow waiting."

"Yes, yes, of course," Zhihao said. "Ask him what he knows about the area or if he has seen anyone else poking around."

Jiayi spoke to the man as best she could. She was far from fluent, but coupling her feeble attempt at communication with hand gestures helped.

"He says that there is a cave to the west, one with an opening shaped like a mouth with teeth, that locals say is cursed, so they stay away from it. He also says there have been other people here, strangers. One a large foreigner with hair like fire."

"Marcus!" Zhihao said.

"He didn't tell him about the cave."

"Lucky for us," Zhihao said.

"He says that every few years, people come to this area looking for something. They never say what and he never tells them about the cave," she explained.

"Why did he tell us?" Zhihao asked.

"He says it's because I'm the only person who ever stopped to talk to him," Jiayi said. "Everyone else just starts digging without permission or pretends they don't see him. His family has herded goats here for centuries, yet the people from the cities act like they don't exist. He says his ancestors provided goat meat and goat milk for the imperial family when they used to go on procession through here."

"That is fascinating," Zhihao said. "Well, after this is over, I would love to come back and talk to him, write some of his stories down."

"He said he would like that very much," Jiayi translated.

They said goodbye to the old man and headed in the direction of the cave.

"That was incredible," Zhihao said. "How did you communicate with him?"

"When I am in someone else's body, I speak in their language, and when they speak to me, I understand it completely. When I wake up, sometimes I remember it. But it is easier if the language is similar to Chinese. I can remember quite a bit from different Chinese dialects. But if a language is too different, like English or French, it is tough for me to remember. I can understand it better than I can speak it."

"You have been in the body of a French woman?" he asked.

"Yes," she said. "The empress has items from all over the world. Sometimes she has me touch them just to verify their origin."

"I can see how that would be a useful gift," Zhihao said. "More and more people are forging antiques because they are worth so much money. Museums and art dealers could use someone with a gift like yours."

Jiayi stopped. "Really?" she asked. "You mean...people would pay me for what I do? Like...like a job?"

"Yes," he said, looking at her. "You would have to be discreet. If the wrong people found out about your gift, they could exploit you or use you in other ways, but for a legitimate art dealer, you would be an invaluable asset."

"Do you know these...art dealers?" she asked.

"I know a few," he said. "I was quite a regular at the British Museum in London."

Jiayi didn't say anything, but she could feel her mouth hanging open. There was so much more she wanted to ask about this. Could he help her get this sort of job? Could she live in London and not have to be a maid? Could he help her escape the empress? She didn't know where to begin.

He reached over and touched her elbow. She looked at him, and his eyes quickly darted to Eunuch Lo. They could not talk about such things in front of him.

"I am sure that the empress greatly values your gift," he said softly.

She nodded. "Indeed. I am very happy to serve the empress."

He nodded, apparently understanding that they would talk about this more at another time. But for now, they needed to find this cave with teeth.

THIRTEEN

They came across a cave that was deep and dark. Even though the sun was shining brightly, they could not see very far in. They would need torches.

"Are you sure this is the right cave?" Jiayi asked.

"No," Zhihao said. "He said a cave to the west, but there are many caves in this area. We will have to start checking them one by one."

Zhihao collected their ropes and tied them together. He then tied one end around a tree and held it as he started into the cave.

"What are you doing?" Jiayi asked.

"This way I won't get lost," he said. "And I'll have something to grab onto in case I fall. Eunuch Lo, you come with me, in case something goes wrong. Jiayi, you stay here for now. I'll yell or send Eunuch Lo back for you once I determine it's safe."

Jiayi couldn't help but feel a little annoyed at being left out, but she nodded. Zhihao was the person in charge, after all.

Zhihao lit two torches and the men entered the cave. It

wasn't long before they and their torchlight were absorbed into the darkness.

Jiayi stood at the edge of the cave, watching intently. She didn't even hear the footsteps behind her.

"Well, well," a familiar voice said. "I was hoping to see you again."

"Marcus!" she gasped as she turned around.

"The one and only," he said with a sweeping, exaggerated bow. "So, what brings you out here?"

"Just...exploring..." she said.

"Now you and I both know that isn't true," he said. "There is no way Teddy would be out here in the middle of nowhere without a solid lead on something specific."

"You...seem to know him quite well," she said.

"Probably better than you," he said. "And you're supposed to be his sister."

Jiayi looked away. It was clear from his tone that he didn't think she was Zhihao's sister. There was no reason for her to reply. Lying further would only make her look like a fool, but telling him the truth could compromise her position.

"You don't have to tell me who you really are," Marcus said. "But I would love to know what you are looking for."

"You know I can't tell you that," she said.

"I can make it worth your while," he said, holding up a gold coin.

"I don't need your money," she said, which was a lie, but seemed to be the right thing to say.

"Then what do you want?" he asked. "You seemed awfully interested in my...business dealings."

Jiayi thought for a moment. She had hoped for a chance to meet with him again and talk more about his business or find out if he could help her get out of the country. Was she now going to be too scared to take that chance?

"I want to leave China," she said quickly. "Go to England. Or America. I don't care which."

"That's...a tall order," Marcus said, rubbing his chin.

"I can pay," she said. "Or, well, I can barter. I have...items I can sell. Or you can sell for me."

"Like what?" he asked.

She reached into her bag with a gloved hand and pulled out one of the empress's combs, the one Eunuch Lo had seen her steal. She had been wanting to get rid of it for as long as she'd had it. It was too dangerous to keep. The comb was studded with jewels that were undoubtedly real. One jewel would probably be worth enough for passage on a ship, and this comb had a dozen jewels studded in it, not to mention the fact that the comb was made of gold.

Marcus whistled. "Hot damn, little mama," he said. "Where did you get something like that?"

"The same place I got this," she said, pulling out the statue she had stolen from him the day before.

Marcus nearly barked a laugh, but caught himself. He shot a look back into the cave, clearly not wanting Zhihao or Eunuch Lo to hear him. He nodded and took the statue from her. "That is one impressive trick. I noticed later that it was missing, but I didn't suspect you in the slightest. I thought I must have just left it on the table by accident. You could make a lot of money with a skill like that."

"I know," she said, recalling her thieving days. "But that's not what I want to do. I just want to get to San Francisco or New York or London and get an honest job. I know you can sell that comb for me and get me the money."

"Not really a matter of money," he said. "It's a legal issue. Lots of borders are closed to Chinese women."

"I'm sure you have means," she said even though she had no idea what legal issues he was referring to.

"That I do, little miss," he said. "But what's in it for me? Like you, I don't need money."

She nodded. "You make the arrangements, and I'll tell you what we are looking for."

"Arrangements aren't an issue," he said. "I know a ship leaving the Tanggu Port in three days." He handed her a small card. "Show my card to anyone at Tanggu, and they will show you which ship is mine."

She took the card and looked at it as if she was reading it. "Thank you," she said. "When I arrive at the ship, I'll tell you what you want to know."

"Fair enough," he said. He opened her hand and placed several coins into it. He closed her fingers around them. "This should be enough if you need to hire a ride to Tanggu." He kissed her closed fingers far more gently than she would have thought possible for a man as large and burly as he was.

"Pleasure doing business with you," he said with a tip of his hat. "And I look forward to much more pleasurable business."

Jiayi blushed and pulled her hand from his. She deposited the coins in her bag. "In three days," she said.

"In three days," he repeated as he walked away.

As soon as he was out of sight, she exhaled. She couldn't believe that she had just made a deal like that with someone who was clearly dangerous. It was exciting. Even though a part of her felt like she had just made a huge mistake, she also felt bold and strong. She had just bargained for her passage out of China. She was going to escape!

Of course, she wasn't sure if she would take him up on

his offer. After all, she had no idea if she could really trust him, if he could actually get her into another country, and what kind of work would be waiting for her. Zhihao had said that he could get her a job at a museum or for an art collector. That would be wonderful. She would have to talk to him more about that. If she could secure help from Zhihao, she wouldn't need help from Marcus. She just wouldn't show up at the Tanggu Port and he could leave without her. He might be angry, but he would get over it. He still had her comb as payment, after all.

Everything seemed to be going wonderfully. She had a feeling they were close to the seal. They would surely find it. And she had two solid leads on leaving China. Her heart beat furiously in her chest. Everything was working out in her favor for once in her life.

FOURTEEN

"Jiayi!" Zhihao said, dropping a hand on her shoulder. She turned to him, startled. "Didn't you hear me calling you?" he asked.

"Sorry," she said. "I...I thought I heard something out that way." She pointed toward a pile of rocks.

"Probably just a snake or rabbit," Zhihao said.

"Did you need something?" she asked. "Did you find anything in the cave?"

He held up some arrowheads. "Just these," he said. "Maybe if you touch them, you'll learn something that could tell us if we are on the right track."

"I don't know," she said, clasping her hands behind her back. "I think I should conserve my energy. Besides, I don't think Lady Cai would come into contact with weapons. I think we should wait. If we don't find anything else, I can try."

"Fair enough," he said, putting the arrowheads into his bag.

"You didn't find anything else in there?" she asked.

He shook his head as he helped Eunuch Lo wind the

rope. "Nothing related to the seal. I did find this, though." He handed her a tin can. She tapped it and then sniffed it, making a face.

"What is it? It smells rancid," she said, handing it back.

"Can of tinned beef," he said. He pointed to the bottom of the can. "Crosse and Blackwell. A British company. Marcus has been here. He might not have found the seal, but he's been here. He's one step ahead of us at least." He sighed in frustration and shook his head.

"Oh dear," Jiayi said. "But you don't think he found the seal?"

He finished winding up the rope. "I don't think so. The cave was nothing special. I found a couple of broken spears. Maybe the rebels who attacked the imperial procession used this cave before or after the attack."

"Then we can still find it first," she said. "But I think we need a better plan than just going from cave to cave hoping to find something."

"I wish I had one," Zhihao said. "But unless you can see something to help us narrow down the search, I don't have a better idea."

Jiayi sighed and sat on a rock nearby. She pulled her folio out of her bag and began flipping through the pages.

"Are those she sketches of your visions?" Zhihao asked, walking over. "Can I have a look?"

Jiayi tilted the pages away from him so he couldn't see and shook her head. "I'd rather you didn't," she said. "They aren't very good. Just let me look for a moment, see if anything stands out to me."

Zhihao put his hands up in surrender and backed away, though now he wanted to see her sketches more than ever. Was she really that self-conscious? Or was she hiding something? Zhihao tried to distract himself while he waited, looking at the various rocks and dead trees that surrounded him, but his eyes kept going back to Jiayi. Her brow wrinkled as she studied the images, her eyes focused. A few wisps of hair framed her face. He wished he had any artistic skill so he could sketch her in this moment. He would have to see if he could procure a camera so he could take a photograph of her. After all, if they did manage to find the seal, they could become famous. It would only be fair if she were pictured by his side as he made the brilliant discovery...

"Here is something," she said, looking up. She stood and handed him a drawing of a landscape. It was quite good, in Zhihao's non-professional opinion, clear and detailed. She could probably be a respected artist if she were given any formal training.

"What are we looking at?" Zhihao asked.

"Here," she said, pointing. "According to my last vision of Lady Cai, she went to a tent and wrote a letter to her brother."

"I remember," Zhihao said. "But you said you didn't see anything useful."

"That's what I thought at the time," she said. "What stood out to me more than anything was the fact that Lady Cai had her own tent at all. She should have been in a tent with the rest of the Inner Court, the other ladies and their children."

"That is true," Zhihao said. "But how does this help us?"

"What if it wasn't her tent?" Jiayi said. "What if it was actually the emperor's tent? She could have been staying with him as his Favored Lady."

"True..." Zhihao said, still not seeing why this was significant.

"Look," she said, handing him the image. "This is how

the tent looked as she approached it. See how one side of the tent is flush against the wall of the mountain pass?"

"Yes," Zhihao said. "That is somewhat odd, I suppose. Usually, an imperial tent would be open on each side so guards could patrol the whole thing."

"If we line up the map and this drawing, there should be a cave right on the other side of that rocky wall."

"You think Lady Cai...dug through the wall and into the cave on the other side to hide the seal?" Zhihao asked, rubbing his chin.

Jiayi sighed and ripped her drawing away. "You're right," she said. "That's stupid."

"No!" Zhihao said, grabbing her arm. "I'm...heh." He couldn't help but laugh a little. "I'm just shocked because it is so brilliant."

"Really?" Jiayi asked, her eyes brightening.

"Well, I don't think she dug through the wall, but the emperor could have ordered someone else to. And as you said, it's a better place to start than just picking random caves. Might as well check that one first."

"Great!" Jiayi said.

Zhihao couldn't help but bask in the warmth of her smile. He had been a teacher for many years, but he didn't enjoy it. He never had any students that stood out to him or surprised him. Jiayi made him feel like a real teacher, a mentor, someone who inspired. In a way, she inspired him. Her zeal for finding the seal and her excitement at every new discovery rekindled a love for archeology he hadn't felt...well, he hadn't felt since he returned to China. In a way, she reminded him of Rebecca. Rebecca also inspired him, though in different ways. No, he couldn't think about her right now. She was long lost to him. He had to let her go.

FIFTEEN

*N*ever had anyone made Jiayi feel so smart and capable. Of course, they most likely wouldn't find anything in the cave, but still, she had examined the evidence and made a reasonable guess that no one else did. And Zhihao praised her for it! This well-educated, world-traveled man had called her brilliant. It almost made up for the time he called her crazy.

Almost.

As they walked to the cave, Jiayi took deep calming breaths and drank plenty of water. If they found anything in the cave, she wanted to have enough strength to see what it could tell her. Her heart raced as they approached the area.

"So according to this map," Zhihao explained, "the back of the cave, where the tent would have been, is to the east of this ridge, but the proper entrance to the cave should be to the west."

"The west would be where the goatherd said there was a cursed cave," Jiayi said. "But would it be better to try to find Lady Cai's entrance?"

"I'm sure that entrance is well hidden," Zhihao said. "It

wouldn't have done much good to leave a big hole in a rock wall leading straight to the seal. The emperor probably had a few trusted men place a large boulder in front of it to seal the entrance."

Jiayi nodded. "Can I go into the cave with you this time?" she asked. "I...I want to be there when you find it." In truth, she didn't want to be left alone again in case Marcus came back or was still watching her. Her earlier confidence after striking a deal with him had worn off a bit. She didn't think she could keep her nerves in check as well as she had before if he spoke to her again.

"Sure," Zhihao said. "But you'll need to stay back, just in case."

Jiayi sighed. "Of course," she said, finding his protective-ness a bit extreme. "Just in case."

As they arrived at the cave, it did look exactly as the goatherd described, like a dragon's mouth with sharp fangs pointing up and down. It was rather fitting, Jiayi thought, since the emperor was represented by the dragon. Though "dragon" is not the way she would describe the current emperor, the empress's nephew. He was a thin waif of a man who spoke softly, if at all. Images of dragons could be found everywhere in the Forbidden City, from wall decorations to food bowls. She also knew that the emperor's seal was adorned with dragons. She had a sketch of it in her notebook.

Zhihao followed the same procedure as before, tying the rope around a nearby tree, and then each of them took hold of it as they entered the cave. Eunuch Lo lit a torch and held it before him. They proceeded into the cave slowly, but had to move even more carefully as they stepped further in. Not far beyond the jagged mouth of the cave, the rocky floor descended quickly. They were soon climbing over boulders and slipping through narrow passages. Jiayi was thankful for the rope. She would have been swiftly lost without it. But then the rope went taut.

"We are going to have to abandon the rope here," Zhihao said. "We've reached the end of it."

"How will we find our way?" Jiayi asked.

Zhihao pulled a stick of chalk out of his pocket. "We will mark the walls with this."

Jiayi breathed a sigh of relief.

"Now, all we have to do is...Ahh!" Zhihao yelled as he lost his footing and fell backward. Where he fell, Jiayi could not tell in the dark. She started to run toward him, but Eunuch Lo placed his hand on her shoulder. He then pointed toward the ground.

It took her a moment, but as she moved her torch and her eyes adjusted, she saw it—a long piece of twine was stretched along the path. She cautiously walked over to where she had last seen Zhihao and called out, moving her torch to and fro.

"Are you all right?" she called out. "Can you hear me?"

"Ah-ahh!" she heard him yell from below.

"What is it?" she asked again, more frantically. "Are you hurt?"

"N...no..." Zhihao groaned. "But I'm not exactly alone down here. There's a dead body."

"What?" Jiayi yelled back, sure she misheard him.

"Don't worry," he said. "The path is just a steep incline here, not a straight drop. You can come down—carefully!"

Jiayi slowly tested each step two or three times as she moved down the incline. She finally made it to Zhihao. He was still sitting on the ground, his white shirt streaked with mud. Next to him was indeed a dead body—what was left of one anyway. It was mainly a skeleton.

"It's all right," he said, seeing her apprehension. "It won't bite."

"Are you sure you are not hurt?" she asked.

"Only my pride," he said as he held his torch to hers to relight it.

"Nonsense," she said as Eunuch Lo appeared next to her and moved a little ways further, closely looking out for more traps. "You tripped over a piece of twine across the path. It wasn't your fault."

"A piece of twine?" he asked as he stood and dusted himself off. "I didn't see a thing. Where would it have come from? Are you sure?"

"Yes," she said. "Eunuch Lo spotted it after you fell."

"The goatherd said that the cave was cursed, right?" Zhihao said more than asked. "If there are traps set in the cave and people have died exploring here, that could have caused the locals to think it was cursed."

"But why would there be traps here?" Jiayi asked.

"Because," Zhihao replied with a smile, "we are on the right track."

Jiayi thought about that for a minute. "So you think Lady Cai hid the seal here and then set the traps to kill anyone who came after it."

"That is my theory," Zhihao said, standing up and rubbing his back. "We can't stop now."

Eunuch Lo took the lead for a while, followed by Zhihao, and finally Jiayi. Eunuch Lo was very thorough as he searched high and low for anything out of place. They moved slowly and surely until Zhihao and Jiayi heard a groan from Eunuch Lo. They all looked up as a string his torch had touched sizzled and snapped. The cave rumbled, and they all hit the ground and covered their heads as several large boulders bounced toward them but glanced off the higher rocks around them and fell down a nearby cliff. They waited until the cave was silent again before moving.

"We are lucky that didn't start a cave-in," Zhihao said.

"Maybe we should head back," Jiayi said. "Maybe the cave *is* cursed. Or maybe it is like the pearl over the emperor's throne—no one should be here except the emperor."

"Don't be silly," Zhihao said. "It's not a curse. The traps were set by humans. We just have to be smarter humans."

Jiayi didn't think it would be that simple. It was easier to set traps than avoid them, she figured. But she didn't really want to go back. She agreed that the cave had to be trapped for a reason. She hung back, though, away from Zhihao and Eunuch Lo as they moved deeper into the cave. They managed to find three more trap triggers, more twine stretching the length of the path high and low, and avoided them. They finally came to a large open cavern. The ceiling had to be dozens of meters high. There was filtered light coming in through small cracks in the far wall that glistened off of the moist stalactites. Jiayi gasped. She had seen many amazing things in her visions, but seeing something so incredible in real life took her breath away.

Zhihao smiled at her. "It never gets old," he said.

"What?" she asked.

"I've been in caves all over the world, yet each one is a marvel of nature."

Jiayi nodded in agreement.

Her wonder quickly soured, though, when she saw that there were several more old skeletons scattered around the room. This place might not be cursed, but it certainly had a foul energy.

But there, in the middle of the room, sitting reverently on a stone pedestal, was a red lacquer box, just like the one that had once held the emperor's seal.

SIXTEEN

"*W*e found it!" Zhihao exclaimed. He couldn't contain his excitement. They found it! Only a few days before, he thought this was nothing but a fool's errand, but now they had actually found the damn thing!

The three of them ran over to it for a closer look. The box looked exactly the same as the one in the empress's possession.

"It can't be the real box," Jiayi said. "The empress has the box."

"But the empress has a fake seal," Zhihao replied. "Maybe she has a fake box."

"No," Jiayi said, shaking her head. "I've traveled all through history with that box. I know it's real."

Zhihao nodded. "You are probably right. But still, this must be where the seal has been hidden all these years."

He reached out to touch the box, but Eunuch Lo grabbed his wrist. "We found many traps in this cave," he said. "The box could be a trap as well."

Zhihao pulled his hand back but leaned in for a closer look. "You may be right," he said. "But I'm not sure we will be able to find out if it is rigged or not without taking a chance."

Jiayi held up her torch and looked around the room. She walked over to the cracked wall and ran her fingers over it. "Do you suppose this is where the emperor originally entered the cave?" she asked. "These rocks don't quite fit together."

Zhihao stood next to her and looked at his map. "Yes, I believe so. The emperor's tent would have been on the other side of this wall."

Jiayi sighed. "It's just so overwhelming," she said. "To be here, where the emperor once stood. Figuring out his greatest secret."

"Well, we haven't figured it out yet," Zhihao said. "First, we need to get the seal out of the box."

"What do you want to do?" she asked.

"Touch the box," he said. "Maybe you will be able to learn whether or not the box is rigged and find out for sure if the seal is inside."

Jiayi nodded. She walked over to the box and took some deep breaths. "Be sure to catch me when I fall," Jiayi said to Zhihao.

"Always," Zhihao said.

Jiayi's heart swelled. She was foolish to think she could ever trust Marcus more than Zhihao. Zhihao was her friend and partner. After this was over, she would tell him everything and get him to help her escape the empress. Maybe he would even go with her.

As Zhihao stood next to her, she took off her gloves, inhaled deeply, and then reached out to touch the box.

*L*ady Cai looked around the cave. The entrance to the cave the men had built was concealed by the emperor's tent, but a dozen torches lit the room bright as day. Several men were centering a large round stone in the room, the one that would hold the fake box for the seal. Or so the minister would think.

The emperor approached her and embraced her warmly, then the emperor kissed her with a hunger.

"What of the rebels?" she asked when the emperor stopped kissing her long enough to take a breath. "Have they been subdued?"

"Easily," he said. "They were just hired thugs meant to menace me so I would have a chance to give you the seal."

"I can't believe Minister Shun thought I would betray you so easily," Lady Cai said.

The emperor gently touched her face. "He doesn't believe that love can be a powerful, protective force. He thinks it is a weakness."

"Your love gives me strength," she said. "Though I am still afraid. He is very powerful."

"I know," he said. "He would do anything to get his hands on it. And after you fail him, who knows who else of my inner circle he will try to enlist. That is why the seal must be hidden. We must keep it safe until I am sure of who I can trust again."

The emperor waved his hand, summoning a young man. He could not have been much more than a teenager, but the family resemblance to Lady Cai was obvious.

"I appreciate you coming," the emperor said. "If my lady trusts you, then I trust you as well."

The boy kowtowed on the dirty ground. "Your faith in me is not misplaced," he said.

"Stand up, brother," the emperor said. He then motioned to Lady Cai.

From the box, Lady Cai removed the seal. In the light from the torches, the seal gleamed like fire. She placed the seal in a simple, unadorned wooden box and handed it to her brother.

"You must tell no one what you do with it, save the emperor himself. Not even me. Do you understand?" she asked.

"I do, dear sister," the boy said, holding out his arms. She gave him the box. He then placed the box in a large sack and covered it with raw wool. If he were stopped, he would look like a simple shepherd.

"Go, and do not return," the emperor said. "One of my men will arm traps leading to the cave's entrance after you have exited."

The boy bowed and backed away from the emperor until he was out of sight, followed by one of the emperor's men. A person was never to turn his back on the emperor.

The emperor placed the empty seal box on the large stone and placed a scroll inside.

"I hope the minister does trace the seal here," the emperor said. "It would serve the traitor right. If only I could see his face."

"You have outsmarted him," Lady Cai said. "He should know better than to try and betray you."

The emperor looked around the room as his men placed the final stones in the way of the entrance from his tent. There was only one small opening left. The man who armed the traps then returned to the room.

"Men," the emperor called out. "Line up." They did as they were told. "You have served me well. Your families will be honored for your service."

"May the emperor live ten thousand years!" they said in unison as they kowtowed.

The emperor then drew his sword and, before the men could react, he began to slaughter them one by one. Lady Cai screamed. The first man never saw the strike coming. The second and third men were too stunned to react. The last two men tried to escape, but there was nowhere to go. The emperor was blocking the way to his tent, but if they ran down the path, they would run into the traps. The men were unarmed as they were only performing physical labor. As the men panicked, the emperor calmly stalked them as a tiger does his prey and cut them down with ease.

Lady Cai was sick with horror. She had no idea he was going to kill the men who helped dig into the cavern and set the traps.

"How could you?" she asked.

"How could I not?" he asked. "It was the only way to protect the secrets of this place. Now only you, I, and your brother know the truth. Is that going to be a problem?" he asked, squeezing her hand tightly.

"No, no, my love," she said, but she knew it was a lie. Their love would never be the same. She had never known the emperor to be so cold, so cruel. Was this the price of power? The price of keeping the throne secure?

"Good," he said. He took her hand and led her through the small opening back to his tent. He then placed the last stone over the opening himself.

*J*iayi's eyes fluttered open. She was lying in Zhihao's arms, and he was looking down at her affectionately.

"Welcome back," he said. "So, is the box rigged? Can we open it?"

She sat up and rubbed her head, which was so overwhelmed with emotion. How could the emperor do that to his own men? She could feel Lady Cai's anguish at instantly falling out of love and into fear of who she thought was her soulmate. Jiayi herself worried about how Zhihao was going to react when he learned the seal was not here. He would not be pleased.

"No. Yes...I don't know. What was the question?" she asked as she tried to stand.

Zhihao held her hands and helped her to her feet. "Is the seal in the box? Is it safe to open?"

"I...I don't know if it is safe to open," she said. "I didn't see him set a trap, but the emperor was...he was frightening."

"What do you mean?" he asked. "Where is the seal?"

"It's not here," Jiayi finally said in a low voice, her head drooping. "He gave the seal to Lady Cai's brother and set this cave up as a diversion, a trap for the minister."

"What?" Zhihao nearly roared, his voice reverberating off the walls.

"I'm sorry," Jiayi said, as though this was her fault.

Zhihao stomped over to the box and threw the lid back. He picked up the scroll that was inside it. He ripped the red silk band off and unfurled the paper.

"Congratulations, Minister," he read aloud. "Your plan to gain control of the seal nearly worked, but the woman who you were sure would betray me saved me instead. It is you who will die this day. Perhaps you should have taken your own advice and never placed your trust in a mere girl."

Zhihao crumpled the paper up and threw it to the

ground. He looked in the box again, gripping its sides. "I can't believe this," he said. "After all that, it's still lost."

"We could still find it," Jiayi said. "He sent it with Lady Cai's brother. If we can find out who her brother was..."

"It doesn't matter!" Zhihao yelled. "He's long dead, whoever he was. He could have hidden it anywhere in China. Anywhere in the world!"

"But we've come this far," Jiayi said. "If we find the brother, we can track more clues. Maybe he told another family member or lover about it. Maybe he left a will..."

"Maybe, maybe, maybe!" Zhihao said. "This whole endeavor is a waste of time. We never should have come here. I wish the empress had never sent for me. I never should have trusted her, never should have believed in..."

"...Me?" Jiayi finished for him.

Zhihao's face went red and he turned away sheepishly. "We should go," he finally said.

As he turned back toward the path, they all heard a clicking sound come from the seal box and then a low rumble.

"What did the letter say?" Jiayi asked, her voice trembling. "'It is you who will die this day.' How would he know that...unless..."

Zhihao sighed. "Unless he set the trap himself."

They all looked up. Far above their heads, they saw a giant boulder swing free. It smashed into what must have been a load-bearing stalactite. As the rock hit it, the whole cave started to rumble and shake and rocks fell all around them.

"Run!" Eunuch Lo yelled as he grabbed Jiayi's arm and pushed her toward the path. They all started running down the path, Zhihao in front, then Jiayi, and Eunuch Lo behind. The ground was slippery and uneven, and the shaking was getting worse. Jiayi was doing her best to keep up, and she was glad to have her thick-soled boots, but she was falling farther behind as they climbed over and under and around the obstructions on the way to the cave entrance.

In their rush, Jiayi forgot about the trap triggers they had avoided on the way in and she tripped over one of the taut pieces of twine.

"Oh no!" she gasped as she looked up and saw a large boulder falling toward her. She scrambled backward but not nearly fast enough.

"Jiayi!" Zhihao called out, but it was too late. He had to move forward, away from her to keep from getting crushed.

Jiayi screamed and held her hands over her head, sure she was about to die, when she felt the strong arms of Eunuch Lo pull her back. He pushed her against the wall and shielded her with his own body as the rock landed with an earth-shattering thud. Jiayi had barely taken a breath when the shaking started again. The rock then fell through the ground as the cavern floor split and the whole cave shifted. When the shaking stopped, Jiayi and Eunuch Lo were on one side of a vast gulf and Zhihao was on the other.

"Oh my god," Jiayi moaned. There was no way she could jump across. If she went back, she would just end up back in the large room, which had most likely collapsed by now. The shaking and rumbling started again as the cave continued to collapse.

"Run!" Jiayi screamed to Zhihao. "Get out of here!"

"Jump!" Zhihao ordered. "You can make it."

"I can't!" she yelled back. The rumbling grew louder and some smaller rocks once again began falling around them.

Jiayi felt Eunuch Lo grab her belt.

"Catch her!" he yelled to Zhihao. Zhihao nodded.

"What?" Jiayi asked, panicked.

"I have fulfilled my promise," Eunuch Lo whispered in her ear. Before she could react, he grabbed her foot and used all his strength to hurl her across the crevasse.

Jiayi stretched her hand out toward Zhihao and was shocked when their fingers touched. She felt Zhihao's hands grip both of her wrists as she kept falling. Her body slammed into the wall of the crevasse, but she had at least stopped falling. She looked up and saw Zhihao straining to hold on.

"Use your feet!" he yelled. "Climb up! Climb up!"

She nodded and did as she was told, quickly finding footholds on the rock wall to shift her weight on to. After only two or three steps, Zhihao was able to lift her over the side of the ravine and back onto the path.

Without thinking, she embraced him, but only for a second. She then stood and looked back across the ravine at Eunuch Lo.

"Jump!" she called to him. "Hurry!"

"Run!" he yelled as more rocks fell, quicker now. Zhihao grabbed her arm and pulled her back down the path as the rocks fell in a deluge. She lost sight of Eunuch Lo.

Jiayi and Zhihao quickly made their way back along the remainder of the path. The temperature rose and sunlight began illuminating the cave. Even though they could still hear the cave falling apart behind them, they were soon safe outside.

SEVENTEEN

*O*nce they were out of the cave, Zhihao and Jiayi both collapsed in relief. They took deep breaths, grateful to be alive. After a minute, Jiayi ran back to the cave entrance.

"Eunuch Lo!" she called out. "Eunuch Lo!" But all she heard was a slight rumbling of the last rocks settling. "What promise?" she screamed.

Zhihao grunted in annoyance. "He's dead, Jiayi!" he snapped, more harshly than he intended.

Jiayi slumped to the ground and began to cry.

"Oh stop," Zhihao said. "You never liked him anyway."

"I didn't want him to die," she said. "Especially not for me! Why would he do that?"

"Don't put too much thought into it," he said. "It was his job to protect you. If you had died and he went back to the empress, she'd have killed him anyway."

"How can you be so heartless?" she asked, tears streaming down her face.

Zhihao ran his hands through his hair in frustration.

"Forget it, Jiayi. Just forget it. Let's go home. I'll be glad to put this whole fiasco behind me."

Jiayi wiped her face as the two of them headed back to camp. Zhihao knew he was acting badly. He shouldn't be so cruel or blame Jiayi for what happened. But the truth was that he was feeling terribly guilty over the death of Eunuch Lo, and it was bringing back horrible memories of his last dig in Egypt and how things had ended with Rebecca. He groaned to himself and walked more quickly back to the camp.

When they arrived, Zhihao started tearing down his tent and packing what he could on his horse.

"Zhihao," Jiayi said softly. "It is already late in the day and we are both exhausted. Should we not stay here for the night?"

"I couldn't stay here another moment," he said. "You do what you want."

"You would...leave me here?" she asked, worry lines creasing her brow.

Zhihao tightened one of his saddle straps. He wanted to be alone. He wanted to ride away by himself and never speak of this misadventure again, but he took a deep breath and stopped himself from saying such out loud.

"Of course not," he said after an unacceptably long pause. "Just pack your things, please, and let's get out of here."

Jiayi turned and did her best to tear down her tent and pack her things. She was clumsy and obviously had no idea what she was doing, but Zhihao couldn't find it in himself to help her. He remembered that it was Eunuch Lo who had built and tore down her tent the past few nights. It was Eunuch Lo who had packed her gear and cooked her breakfast. As a lady raised in the palace, Jiayi had not been taught a single life skill. She would surely die if he left her to her own devices.

"If we ride hard," Zhihao said as they both finally mounted their horses, "we should be able to make it back to the inn."

He didn't explain further, and she did not respond, but it was implied that by making it back to the inn, Jiayi would have somewhere to sleep and be able to get food without having to rely on someone else. Zhihao hoped Jiayi took it as his way of being kind and not an insult, but he couldn't bring himself to explain further.

They rode back to the town and the inn without speaking. When they arrived, Zhihao ordered them each a bath, a room, and a meal. When they saw each other at dinner that night, near midnight, they both looked clean, but still physically and emotionally worn. As they picked at their rice and vegetables, it was Jiayi who finally spoke first.

"I know you don't want to talk to me," she said, "but I need to know more about what we spoke of yesterday, about getting a job in America or England. I...I don't want to go back to the empress. Especially since we...since *I* failed. I'm not sure I can face her."

"You don't have a choice," Zhihao said. "I don't know what I was thinking. I can't get you a job. You don't have any education and no one will believe in your 'powers.'"

"But you said—"

"I wasn't thinking clearly," Zhihao interrupted. "I was just...caught up in the excitement of the moment or something. But after...after what happened, I realize that I have no idea what we are dealing with here. I mean, what are you even? Is any of this even real? I..." He dropped his chopsticks and rubbed his face, not sure if he should laugh or cry. "I don't know. I just don't know. I don't know what happened back there. I don't know what is going to happen for myself next. I can't even be bothered to try and think about you right now. I just need to go back, get back to work, get back to...to reality for a while and then, maybe later, after I've had some distance, maybe then I can think of what to do."

"You can't be bothered?" she asked incredulously. "This is my life we are talking about. Do you know what the empress will do to me?"

"And me!" Zhihao exclaimed. "You aren't the only failure here. The empress is going to have my neck!"

"We both know that isn't true," Jiayi said.

"She's going to be furious," Zhihao said.

"But she won't kill you," Jiayi said. "You are a man, one she already invested heavily in by sending you overseas for your education. You are well respected at the university, very well known. It's why you were selected for this mission. And you were favored by Prince Gong, a man the empress respects to this day. Yes, she will be angry, but you will survive. Your career will survive. You have a family that loves you and friends to support you. But what about me?

"Outside the Inner Court, no one even knows I exist. Even among the ladies, I'm no one, just a dirty little street urchin who can't even read." She gasped as though trying to stop the tears from flowing.

Zhihao put his hand to his mouth. She couldn't read? A street kid? He knew she had grown up poor, but he didn't realize she meant that poor. Even the empress had come from a poor family, but they were from a noble lineage and had been able to present her as a gift to the emperor when it was time for the consort selection. He assumed Jiayi had a similar background—poor yet respectable.

"I'm nothing but a *gongnu*, a palace slave," she said. "The empress could kill me with her own two hands and would be within her right to do so as my owner. So, forgive me if I don't have the luxury of being angry about going back empty handed like you. I'm terrified."

Zhihao couldn't even look at her, but he could feel her trembling. Her shaking hands were vibrating the table. Zhihao couldn't speak. He knew anything he said would be wrong. He didn't know where to begin. At least he now had a more clear understanding of where she was coming from, why she was upset, but that didn't change the fact that he didn't think he could help her. If he did help her in the way she wanted, whisking her off to a foreign land, the empress would certainly want him dead—and that was no exaggeration. He didn't have the means to anyway. He couldn't get her permission to enter another country. And there was no way he could get her a job. He had been crazy to think he could. He did want to help her, but he had no idea how. He needed time to think of a plan.

"Jiayi," he finally said, reaching across the table and placing his hard on hers. He felt her trembling subside. "I'm sorry. I'm sorry I have not been more sympathetic. But I'm even more sorry that I don't know how to help you."

This time Jiayi could not staunch the tears. She pulled her hand away, putting it to her mouth.

"I'm sorry," he said again. "I don't know what else to say. I just need time—"

Jiayi stood up and flew up the stairs to her room. He had wanted to tell her that he needed time to figure out what to do, but she hadn't given him a chance.

He decided not to chase after her. She was upset and needed to be alone. Hell, he felt the same way. It was now the wee hours of morning and they had been through hell.

Maybe if he got a few hours of sleep, he could think more clearly and come up with a plan.

He left his uneaten bowl of food on the table and slumped up the stairs to his room. He kicked off his boots and fell onto the bed fully dressed. He was asleep in moments.

"*C*an you believe it?" Eli asked, holding up a lantern. "Actually inside the tomb of a king."

Zhihao sighed with satisfaction and took in the sight. They were deep inside the Great Pyramid of Giza. Even though the pyramid had already been discovered and excavated, Eli was there to examine the pyramid from an engineering standpoint so people could better understand how the pyramid had been constructed. They were in the lowest accessible area of the pyramid, very nearly at its base.

"Do you see this here?" Eli asked, pointing to a corner that to anyone else would seem an utterly mundane meeting of two stones, but to Eli told an elaborate story.

"See the two smaller stones on the right side of the joint but the one large stone on the left side?" he asked. Zhihao nodded. "Clearly an imperfection. If the pyramid had been divinely designed and built, God would not make such mistakes."

"You might be a heretic, but at least you aren't irreverent," Zhihao joked.

Eli laughed. "Let's just hope the scholars back home agree with you," he said. "Not only does this prove that the pyramid was made by a human engineer not so unlike myself, but I believe there were at least two engineers, perhaps two designers of this pyramid."

"Why do you think that was?" Zhihao asked.

"You're the historian," Eli said. "Hopefully you can find some documents to support my claims. Perhaps the first engineer couldn't work out the details, or he displeased the pharaoh and had to be replaced."

"Your sister is the linguist," Zhihao said. "Once we determine if it is safe to get a crew down here maybe she can interpret the hieroglyphics. Maybe the engineers included their own story in the pharaoh's journey to the afterlife."

"Speaking of my sister..." Eli said, waggling his eyebrows.

"Not now," Zhihao said. "We should focus on our work."

Eli laughed and turned back to examine the wall further. Zhihao walked back toward the entrance and barked orders at some of the workers.

"That's right, move those support beams over there. We need this place secure by tomorrow so the team can get started," he said.

The workers quickly brought in the beams and began putting them in place. Zhihao reached into his pocket and pulled out a handkerchief Rebecca had given him that was laced with her perfume. He held it to his nose and breathed in deeply. The scent nearly transported him back to her side. Even though she was just topside, he couldn't wait to bring her down into the pyramid. He loved working with her. Rebecca was not just his lover, his little woman waiting at home, but his partner and workmate. Working together side by side on expeditions or research gave his life such a fullness.

One of the workers called out to him, but he waved him off. He wandered over and looked at some of the hieroglyphs on the wall of two birds soaring together. He would have to remember to ask Rebecca what they represented.

"Sir! Sir!" one of the workers called out. "Sir, the beam!"

Zhihao turned back around just as the ground started to shake. He looked up and saw that the workers had placed one of the beams in the wrong place and it had smacked against a load-bearing stone near the top of the chamber. The shaking increased and smaller rocks began to fall, followed suddenly by some larger ones.

"Cave in!" one of the workers yelled, causing a panic as everyone headed for the exit.

"Get out!" Zhihao yelled. He headed for the exit, but stopped to help the workers escape one at a time through the small doorway. After the last worker was out, he glanced around. "Anyone else there?" he called out. He saw a shimmer of light and thought he saw a hand move.

"You there!" he called, and he thought he heard a groan. *Damn*, he thought. Someone must have been stupid enough to get trapped.

"Sir! Sir!" one of the workers called from the doorway. "You must come!"

"Someone is trapped down here!" he yelled back. He gritted his teeth and ran to the light. When he saw what had happened, his heart stopped.

"Eli!" he yelled and went to his friend's side. Eli's legs were trapped under a huge boulder. He had not seen such a large stone fall, but it must have shifted just enough to catch Eli unawares.

Eli grabbed Zhihao's hand and grunted. "You must go!" Eli said. "I'm done for!"

"No!" Zhihao yelled, holding his friend's hand tight. "I'll not leave you." He pushed against the stone but could not budge it an inch, much less lift it to free his friend.

"You must go!" Eli said. "Now!"

The shaking became greater and ever-larger rocks began to fall.

"She cannot lose both of us! Go!"

Zhihao, with tears streaming down his face, left his friend there in the cave.

They never found his body.

Z hihao awoke, drenched in sweat. The same dream over and over again plagued him, especially in times of stress. He sat up and ran his fingers through his hair. Well, she had lost both of them, hadn't she? Eli died that day, and not long afterward, Zhihao returned to China. He had lied to her. He never even wrote to her, not once. He was a coward. He couldn't face her, even on paper. He couldn't live with the guilt. Even though she didn't blame him, she was Eli's sister, and Zhihao could not look at her without seeing his friend's helpless eyes staring back.

The sky was the cool grey of the sun just starting to rise. Had he managed to sleep a few hours? It didn't feel like it. He felt worse than before. He didn't care for Eunuch Lo, but he was reacting the same way as he had after Eli's death. He was taking his guilt and anger out on the woman closest to him. He knew it was wrong. He had to stop. This time, he had to help her.

He still didn't have a plan, but perhaps he and Jiayi could come up with something together. After all, he had to acknowledge that they had worked well together so far.

He put on his shoes and then walked down the hall to her room. He knocked softly so as not to disturb the other guests.

"Jiayi," he called. There was no answer. She was probably still angry with him. He knocked again.

"Jiayi, can we talk, please? I know I was terrible, but I'm sure we can work things out."

He waited, but still, there was no answer. His heart began to race. He shouldn't have let her room alone. Even though it would have been improper for them to room together, she was vulnerable. Without Eunuch Lo here to protect her, any man could have broken into her room in the night. She could have been kidnapped. She had also been upset—terrified, in her words. Would she hurt herself if it kept her from having to face the empress?

He banged on the door. "Jiayi, open this door right now," he ordered.

Just then, the innkeeper came up the stairs, shushing him. "You'll wake the whole house," she admonished.

"Use your key," he said. "She could be hurt."

"Young miss isn't hurt," the old woman said. "She's gone. She left as the cock crowed."

"What?" he yelled. "Open this door!"

The innkeeper pulled out her collection of keys and waved for him to be quiet.

Zhihao had barely heard the lock click when he burst through the door. Sure enough, the girl was gone.

EIGHTEEN

*O*nly a few minutes after Jiayi had returned to her room, she heard the door to Zhihao's room slam shut. What an irritating, selfish, useless boor he was!

Jiayi reached into her bag and pulled out her dragon and phoenix necklace. She laid on her bed and held the necklace to her chest.

She opened her eyes in her favorite place, the arms of Prince Junjie. He was cradling her face in his hands and kissing her. She wrapped her arms around him and kissed him with abandon. She then realized that they were laying down. She moved her leg, wrapping it around his. They were naked and in bed together. She was sandwiched between a cool silk sheet and the prince's hot body.

"How did I get so lucky?" she asked. She couldn't believe that she had awoken precisely where she wanted to be.

"I think I'm the lucky one," he said. "You are the one happiness in my life."

"I am sorry to hear of your troubles, my love," she said.

He sighed and laid his head on her chest. She combed her fingers through his long hair and held him. Even though she had come here to be comforted by him, she was glad he found respite in her arms as well.

"What I wouldn't do for us to be together," he said. "But I am starting to fear for your safety."

"My safety?" she asked.

"Do not worry," he said, smiling up at her. "Forget I said anything. I don't want any of the troubles of the world in here. When we are here, there is only you and me."

"If only the whole world was just you and me," Jiayi said.

"The sun is rising," he said, glancing toward the window. "I must leave soon."

Jiayi nodded but held him even tighter. "Just stay as long as possible," she said. "Just hold me..."

When Jiayi opened her eyes again, her cheeks were wet. Prince Junjie gave her comfort and hope, but leaving him often left her more despondent than when she arrived.

Jiayi sat up, swinging her legs off the bed. She placed the necklace back into her bag and some of the gold coins there clinked. She pulled them out and felt the cool metal in her palm. She was tired of being scared, being hopeless, being sad. There was nothing she could do about Prince Junjie. She knew he was not real, not here. And now, she couldn't rely on Zhihao either.

Well, if Zhihao wouldn't help her, that was just fine. She wasn't so useless. She could save herself. She already *had* saved herself. She still had two more days to get to the Tanggu Port and board Marcus's ship. Soon, she would be on her way to America—without Zhihao's help.

She put her few belongings back in her pack. Among the items was Zhihao's pocket watch. She considered leaving it, leaving all trace of Zhihao behind her. How angry would he be when he found it? Or would he feel gratified?

Justified in believing she was not worth his time? Just a stupid little thief. No, she would not give him the satisfaction. She stuffed the pocket watch into her bag and silently slipped through her door. As she passed by Zhihao's room, she could hear him snoring. While part of her was glad, since it meant she would be long gone by the time he woke, part of her was hurt. How could he sleep so soundly after the fight they just had? He was a selfish pig.

Jiayi went to the dining hall, where she found the innkeeper, who was still cleaning up after the guests.

"Dear auntie," Jiayi said, calling the woman auntie as a polite and friendly form of address. "Do you never sleep?"

The woman chuckled. "What is sleep? And what of you? Hungry now? You didn't eat your supper. You are too skinny!"

"I can't eat," Jiayi said. "I...I need help. I need to..." Even though she had already been speaking in a low voice, she leaned in and whispered. "I need to escape that man."

The innkeeper pursed her lips and nodded her head. No doubt in her line of work, she had seen many scared young women brought through. Girls being bought, sold, and traded. None of whom she could help.

"You know I need his permission," the woman said. "You are his property."

"But I'm not," Jiayi said. "Do you remember the other man I was with? The tall one? I was with him. He was my protector. But he...he was killed yesterday. So now I'm only with this man, and I'm scared. Please, please help me, auntie."

The woman sighed. Jiayi knew she had put the woman in a bad position. If she helped her, Zhihao could sue the woman for stealing his property. But Jiayi had a feeling that Zhihao wouldn't do that. He could never admit to the empress that he had lost her. He would rather flee the country than face her wrath.

The woman finally nodded. "What do you need?"

Jiayi handed her Marcus's card. "I need to get here," she said. "As quickly as possible."

The woman nodded. "My neighbor, he will be taking a cartload of silk to the port to ship to the West. He should be leaving any moment. Follow me."

The two quietly exited the inn and walked down the road a ways. They soon came upon a man who was about to climb up into a loaded down cart that was harnessed to two horses. The man must have been quite prosperous to be able to own horses instead of donkeys to pull his goods. The innkeeper explained to the man what was going on, but they spoke in a regional dialect Jaiyi couldn't quite understand. He nodded as the innkeeper spoke, and then the two had a lively exchange. Finally, the innkeeper explained to Jiayi what was going on.

"He says he needs a payment to take you. Even though he is going that way, the stubborn ass says he is not a free donkey cart."

"Of course," Jiayi said. She had no idea how much she should pay him out of the money Marcus had given her. She had not bought anything in years. She reached into her bag and pulled out one of the gold coins.

"Is this enough?" she asked.

The man took the coin quickly and bit it between his teeth. He nodded.

Jiayi then reached into her bag and pulled out two more coins. She slipped them to the innkeeper and then hugged her.

"Little sister!" the innkeeper gasped. "I cannot take this! People will think I stole it."

Jiayi wrapped her hands around the coins. "It is less than you deserve," she said.

The woman started to protest, as was only polite, but they didn't have time. The horses were growing restless, and the cart driver was impatient. Jiayi turned around and climbed up into the cart.

"Thank you for your help," Jiayi said. The woman nodded and the two held hands for as long as they could as the cart pulled away. Jiayi had been shown kindness from so few people in the world, she was certain she would never forget this woman.

*T*he cart driver was shipping precious cargo. So precious, he could not rest. If he left his cart for even a moment, thieves could swoop in and steal the expensive silk. Because of this, they did not stop to sleep at night. They only stopped twice along the way to get fresh horses. He was kind enough to let Jiayi sleep in the back with the bolts of silk, when her emotions were calm enough to let her rest anyway. He did not sleep, but he did let Jiayi take the reins and drive the horses a few times, which she enjoyed.

When they arrived at the port, she checked her bag for the card with Marcus's information on it and could not find it.

"I must have dropped it or left it with the innkeeper," Jiayi said.

"No trouble," the silk cart driver said. "I remember what it was called. The ship you want was called the *Pandora*. It is at East Dock."

"Thank you so much!" she said and headed east.

The dock was bustling with activity. There were thousands of people, donkeys and horses pulling carts, towers of boxes, even cages full of animals. She was shocked to see large birds, much taller than a man, with long rope-like necks and huge glass eyes. They would bite people who got too close. In another cage, she saw a tiger pacing. The bars were too close together for him to stick his paws through, but he roared ferociously. She was surprised to see so many women around her. Some of them were selling food or other goods to the sailors, some of them were trying to get the men to follow them somewhere, and some of the women Jiayi could swear were sailors themselves, working to ready the ships to sail. She even saw foreign women. White women in tight gowns holding umbrellas and dark brown women in long flowing robes.

The ships themselves were what amazed Jiayi more than anything. Even in her dreams, she had never seen ships like these. They were as large as buildings with spires that reached up to the sky. She couldn't wait to climb aboard one. Her heart beat fast in her chest. A whole new adventure was awaiting her!

She still wasn't sure where the ship was, so she asked a few people as she made her way down the dock. Finally, she saw Marcus himself. He was hard to miss! He was standing on a large crate, barking orders to the coolies around him who were moving bags and boxes onto the ship. She waved, and Marcus saw her. He smiled as he jumped down and approached.

"You came!" he said. "I was beginning to worry."

"It was harder to get away from Zhi...Teddy than I expected," she said.

"Did you find what you were looking for?" he asked her.

She shook her head. "No," she said. "We failed."

"Will you tell me what you were looking for, then?" he asked.

"Once we are on the ship," she said. "It's a long story. I'll tell you everything."

His expression darkened for a moment, but then he smiled and placed his hand on her arm. "Well, right this way," he said, motioning to the ship.

Now that she took a moment to look at the ship, she was a little disappointed. It was rather small compared to the other ships along the dock. It also seemed to be in a bit of disrepair. It needed a paint job and some of the sails were ratty. As she neared the gangplank, though, she froze. She was able to see through some of the portholes below deck and knew something was wrong. Through the portholes, women were screaming and waving their arms. They were calling for help.

"What...what is the meaning of this?" Jiayi asked, stepping away from Marcus.

"Nothing," he said. "Just a bit of side business."

"Nothing?" she asked. "Women are nothing?"

"It is nothing that needs to concern you," he said, then he turned and yelled at the women. "Shut up, you bitches!" The women quieted...for a moment.

"But what are you doing with them?" she asked. "A... side business? What do you mean?"

"It's just some brides bound for America," he said. "They are just scared of their new lives. Come on. I can explain more later, just as *you* can explain more." He gripped her arm and pulled her toward the gangplank.

Her heart beat fast, but this time from fear. If she fought him, he could forcibly take her, and then consider her an enemy. If she went willingly, he could still live up to his end of the bargain. But why should she trust him at all? She was such an idiot!

She looked up on the deck and saw a Chinese man in a crisp white suit looking down at her. When their eyes met, he quickly moved out of sight. Why would a man like that be on the ship?

Just then, a white man walked up to the gangplank with several Chinese women in tow, all chained together.

"Why are they in chains?" Jiayi asked frantically.

"Help us!" one of the women yelled when she saw Jiayi, and the others then chimed in.

"Help me!"

"I've been kidnapped!"

"Where am I?"

They reached out to her with shackled wrists, tears streaming down their faces.

Jiayi knew then that she had to escape. She didn't think she could help the women since their wrists and ankles were clapped in irons, but she could help herself. She had to run.

She turned away from Marcus, trying to slip from his grasp, but he was too strong. He held her wrist tightly and then gripped her forearm with his other hand.

A memory flashed in her mind. She looked Marcus in the face, her eyes narrow and her jaw set tight. She placed her free hand on his arm and used his body as leverage. She swung her right leg up in the air, putting the weight of her whole body behind the kick. Her heel connected with Marcus's face with such force, and he was in such shock, that he immediately let her go and stumbled back. Jiayi landed on her feet and turned to run.

She collided with Zhihao.

"Jiayi!" he exclaimed. "What was...how did..." he sputtered, unable to put his thoughts into words.

She tried to run past him, but he held her arm. She quickly spun her arm in a circle, releasing it from his grip. As he tried to grab her again, she lifted her hand and deflected him. He looked at her, confused, and she narrowed her gaze, telling him with her eyes not to grab her again. He seemed to get the message because he held up his hands in defeat.

"Please, just listen to me," he said. "Don't run. Let me help you."

A large hand then landed on Zhihao's shoulder. He turned around and Marcus was standing there.

"I don't know what the hell's going on," Marcus yelled. "But we had an agreement. The girl comes with me."

"No way, Marcus!" Zhihao said. "Let her go or you'll lose *all* your cargo." He motioned to the women who were being dragged up the gangplank. "Would be terrible if someone alerted customs before you had a chance to raise anchor."

"You better both get out of here," Marcus growled. "But you've made a powerful enemy today, *friends*."

He didn't have to tell Jiayi twice. She quickly slipped through the crowd. She chanced a glance back to make sure Marcus wasn't following her and saw that Zhihao was nearly on her heels. Over her shoulder, she looked back at the *Pandora*. The man in a white suit had rushed down the plank and was arguing with Marcus. The more she thought about it, the more stupid and terrified she felt. She had almost made a fatal error. The only thing worse was that Zhihao had been present to learn about what she had done. She was sure he would never let her live it down.

NINETEEN

*a*s they left the dock and ended up back on the main cobbled stone road, Zhihao placed his hand on Jiayi's back.

"What are you doing here?" she finally asked.

"I came to rescue you," he said.

"I can handle myself," she said. "I had already decided to leave before you showed up."

"I noticed," he said. "What was that anyway? How did you learn to do that?"

"Remember how I told you that I sometimes remembered languages from my dreams? Sometimes I remember...other things as well."

"You learned how to fight in one of your dreams?" he asked. "I thought you could only be women in your dreams."

"Women can fight too," she said indignantly, "as you just saw. I was once a woman who studied Wushu on Song Mountain."

Zhihao could hardly believe what he was hearing, but

he had seen her kick Marcus in the face with his own eyes. What other abilities had she picked up?

"For someone with no education, plans, or prospects, you are quite adept at survival. How did you even know Marcus would be here?" Zhihao asked.

Jiayi sighed and shook her head. "I'll never tell you everything, Zhihao," she said. "Secrets keep me safe. They keep me alive."

"Look," Zhihao said, turning her toward him, but she still refused to look him in the face. "I'm sorry about what happened. I know I was terrible to you. I'm sorry. I...I enjoyed working with you, and I had come to consider you a friend. I betrayed that friendship. I was wrong."

Jiayi didn't respond, but she at least looked less angry than she did before. She sighed and looked longingly back toward the port.

"I can't help you get on a ship," Zhihao said. "But if you come with me, we will figure out a way to help you."

Jiayi nodded. "It would seem I have no choice," she said.

Zhihao took her chin in his hand and forced her to look at him. "Jiayi," he said. "I don't want you to come with me as a last resort, as your only alternative to certain death or poverty. I want you to come with me because I am your friend. I know I do not deserve your trust, but if you come with me, I will do everything in my power to earn that trust back."

Jiayi nodded and gave him a wan smile. "I...I know. I am still hurt, but I will go with you so we can figure this out together—as a team."

If it had been socially acceptable, Zhihao would have hugged her.

"*I* cannot believe you brought her here," Zhihao's mother scolded as they looked through a window into the courtyard of their home and watched Jiayi sketch.

"I had nowhere else to go, Mother," Zhihao said. "I couldn't take her to an inn, or anywhere else alone. The empress would never believe she was...as I found her when she returned."

"So, you bring her here? Endanger all of our lives? What will the empress do when she finds her here?" his mother asked frantically.

"I don't know," Zhihao said, rubbing his forehead. "I have no idea how to find the seal and no way to get her out of the country."

"You should put yourself and your family first," his mother said. "Let the empress have her maid back and do not worry yourself."

"I cannot do that, Mother," he said. "I promised I would protect her."

His mother sighed and teetered over to the stove to remove a teapot from atop a small flame. Like most Han women of high class, her feet were bound. Zhihao had told her everything—almost. He didn't tell her about Jiayi's powers, but he did tell her about the seal and his failure to find it. He was his mother's youngest child, so she doted on him. His father had been ill when he was a boy, so he was closest with his mother. When he was separated from her at age twelve to study abroad, he grieved the separation heavily. The one thing that made him happy about returning to China was seeing his mother again. He had to admit that he was not sure he could leave China again as long as she was alive.

"What if you married her?" his mother asked. "Then her ownership would transfer to you. You could protect her then."

"She is Manchu," Zhihao said. "Manchu are forbidden from marrying Han Chinese."

"The empress recently issued an edict stating that inter-marriage was now legal," his mother said.

"And how many people have taken advantage of that pronouncement?" Zhihao asked. "It might be law on paper, but not in practice yet. I'm not sure I want to be the first to test that new law just to steal her maid. Besides, as the empress's property, the empress has to approve her marriage. I would be a thief, and worse, a traitor if I married her."

"You have gotten yourself into quite a predicament," his mother said as she prepared a tea tray.

"I can't believe you would allow me to marry a maid anyway," Zhihao said with a smirk.

"It could be worse," his mother said. "At your age, my fear of you never marrying is stronger than my need for a good match. At least she is beautiful. And Chinese…"

Zhihao pursed his lips. He was not the first—or only—man educated in England to fall in love with a foreign girl. At least he had the good sense not to marry Rebecca and bring her home as some other men had, much to the horror of their families. Not that he didn't want to. But there was just too much pain, too much history between them. Where was she now? What was she doing? Did she think about him as much as he thought about her? He couldn't believe that Jiayi had seen through her eyes, felt what she felt. Could she do it again? Could she see what Rebecca was doing now? Would he ever get the courage to write to her? To get over her?

"Here, take this out to her," his mother said, breaking into his thoughts. "See what she thinks you should do."

Zhihao nodded and took the tray outside. As he approached Jiayi, he was struck by how lovely she looked. She was once again wearing a Manchu style gown, but still wore her hair in a simple braid. She was sitting on a bench under a cherry blossom tree hunched over her drawing pages. Her cheek was smudged with charcoal and some strands of hair fell around her face. For the first time in days, she looked at peace.

"Can I help you?" she asked, looking up at him.

"Oh, sorry, yes. My mother thought you would enjoy some tea," he said.

"Your mother is so kind," Jiayi said as she straightened her papers and closed her notebook.

Zhihao sat next to her and placed the tea tray between them. He dropped some tea leaves into two cups and then poured hot water over them. He handed her a cup and she held it gently in her fingers as she waited for the leaves to steep and the water to cool.

"I hope your mother does not mind my presence," Jiayi said. "I am very grateful she is allowing me to stay here."

"She likes you very much," Zhihao said. "She even suggested I marry you."

Jiayi let out a small laugh. "So silly, yet kind."

Zhihao wasn't sure what she meant by that. Of course, there were half a dozen reasons why they could not marry, but he wasn't sure if she was calling the reasons why they could not marry silly or the whole idea of them marrying. He wasn't sure himself. They barely knew each other, they certainly weren't in love, and there would be no benefits for his family if he married her. She had no family connections or money. But still, he couldn't help but feel slightly disheartened at her dismissal of the idea.

"Silly," Zhihao repeated as he looked into his teacup. "Indeed."

"So," Jiayi began, "what is the plan?"

"I...I still have no plan," Zhihao said. "I have spoken to a few friends I could trust and none of them think they could help smuggle you to the West safely. You would most likely be caught and sent back. The empress would certainly find out about your attempt. There are some smugglers who specialize in 'paper daughters,' but that is very risky, expensive, and difficult, with no guarantee of success..."

"Maybe we should just keep looking for the seal," Jiayi said. "I feel like we were so close. If we keep looking—"

"Jiayi," Zhihao said with a sigh. "I agree that finding the seal would be the best way out of this situation, but I have no idea where to begin."

"Maybe...maybe I should return to the empress after all," Jiayi said. "You said that there are no records of the details of the Inner Court, yet I know they exist. The Ministry of Household Affairs takes meticulous notes on everything from every coin spent to when each woman is in her moon phase. I believe it has always been so. Those records have to be somewhere."

"They could have just been destroyed," Zhihao said. "What purpose would the ministry have for keeping them?"

"I don't know, but destroying them seems such a waste," Jiayi said, becoming more animated. "Perhaps they are not in any public archive because many people see them as useless. But maybe they are just locked away, forgotten somewhere in the Forbidden City. The palace has ten thousand rooms. There are endless places where something could be forgotten or lost. If I can find the records dating back to the Daoguang Emperor, maybe I can learn more about Lady Cai and her family."

"You said, that night at the inn, that you couldn't read," Zhihao said as gently as he could. "How will you find the right records if you can't read?"

"You could teach me," she said. "I want to learn, so why not?"

"I would be happy to teach you to read," Zhihao said. "But it takes a long time, and we need a plan now. If we return to the Forbidden City empty handed, what will you tell the empress?"

Jiayi sighed and leaned back against the tree. "I don't know."

Their conversations seemed to run in this same circle with no end. Zhihao decided to change the topic of conversation. Maybe a distraction would clear their thoughts.

"What are you working on?" he asked her, reaching for her notebook.

"Oh." She moved the pages out of his reach. "Nothing, just some sketches from my dreams I wanted to get on paper before I forgot them."

"Let me see," he said. "That one you did of the Conghua Pass was wonderful. Show me some others."

"I certainly don't think they are wonderful," she said. "But if I agree, you must promise not to laugh."

"I won't laugh," he said.

She slowly opened her notebook and showed him the first one. It was a detailed drawing of a necklace of a dragon and a phoenix.

"That is a beautiful necklace," he said.

"It isn't from my dreams, but is an artifact the empress once had me use. It's from the Tang Dynasty. She was trying to reach Wu Zetian," Jiayi explained.

"Empress Wu?" Zhihao asked. "The only true empress of China?"

"Yes," Jiayi said. "I'll tell you a secret. The empress is obsessed with Empress Wu."

"Makes sense," he said. "I'm sure she would love to use the precedent of Empress Wu to legitimize her own rule."

"Exactly," Jiayi said.

The next drawing was of a man even Zhihao had to admit was beautiful.

"Who is this charming devil?" Zhihao asked.

"That is..." Jiayi paused for a moment. "Oh, Prince Junjie. I think he is a nephew of Empress Wu."

Zhihao laughed. "Did you really almost forget his name? Come now, even without seeing this image, I know he was handsome. His good looks are legendary."

"Really?" Jiayi asked. "What do you know about him?"

"Oh, he was known as a pretty face, but he was quite skilled in battle as well. He had to wear a terrifying demon mask to scare his enemies in battle because without it, they would not take him seriously as an opponent. I'm glad to see he was just as good looking as the legend says."

He looked up at Jiayi, and she was smiling so wide he thought her eyes would pop out of her head.

"What?" he asked. "Why does this make you so happy?"

"He...he doesn't," she said, shaking her head. "You just get so excited when you talk about history. I love hearing it. I wish I could get that passionate about something."

"I'm sure you will eventually find your calling," he said. "Come, show me the next."

"Umm..." As she rifled through some of the pages, as if looking for something special, one of the papers slipped out of the stack and landed on the ground. As Zhihao leaned down to pick it up, it was if all time stopped. He was looking at some sort of object, square with a carved dragon on top. He knew he had seen the object before.

"Jiayi..." he whispered as he picked up the drawing. "What...what is this?"

"That's the emperor's seal," she said. "Haven't you seen it before?"

"I...no. Of course not," Zhihao said. "I'm not a member of the court. I've never seen the empress stamp an edict before. Everyone in China, probably the world, has heard of the emperor's seal, but no one outside of the empress's inner circle has ever seen it...Except...I *have* seen this."

"What?" Jiayi asked, moving closer to him and staring at the image. "Where?"

Zhihao couldn't believe what he was looking at, but he knew he was right. It was almost too easy, too good to be true. The carved jade dragon on the gold and blue cloisonné base. He felt like an idiot for not recognizing it before.

"The brother, do you know what he looked like? Have you drawn him? I must see his face," Zhihao said.

Jiayi opened her notebook and flipped through the images, finally pulling one out. "Here, this is him, standing to the right of the pedestal. To the left is the Daoguang Emperor," she said, pointing at the figures in the image.

Zhihao laughed. He stood and put his hands to his head. He wanted to scream, he couldn't believe it. That face, those eyes, that man. He knew him.

"I know where it is!" he finally said, pulling Jiayi up to him, her papers scattering on the ground. He hugged her and then spun her around in a circle.

"Know where what is?" Jiayi asked.

"I know where to find the emperor's seal!"

TWENTY

Jiayi was nervous as she climbed the stairs to the library at Peking University. She wasn't sure why. Zhihao was so excited, he bounded up the stairs two at a time. Jiayi was once again dressed as a Manchu lady and had to walk much more cautiously in her pot-bottom shoes as she held the hem of her long gown aloft. As they walked through the campus, everyone stared at them. No doubt they were not used to seeing a woman at the school, especially not one dressed as a lady.

Zhihao was already at the top of the stairs, waving for her to join him. "Hurry!" he called out. "We have no time to waste."

Even though Jiayi wanted to find the seal as much as he did, she had a feeling it was her life that was about to change forever, not his. She wasn't sure if she was terrified of that prospect or wanting to prolong the moment, but neither possibility spurred her to move faster. Her heart was beating like a running horse and her mouth was dry. She licked her lips as she ascended the final step of the

European style building that seemed out of place northwest of Peking.

As they entered the library, Jiayi was struck by the sight of so many books. The walls must have been a dozen meters high and each one covered with books and scrolls. So much knowledge in one place. Would it be possible to ever read all there was to read? If only she could read even one of them...

Jiayi followed Zhihao past many shelves to the back of the library and a dark, dusty corner. There, on a shelf amid a clutter of other items, was the emperor's seal.

Zhihao could not help but laugh as he pulled it down and cradled it close like a child. "I saw this the day we met," he said. "After I saw you, I came here to speak with my mentor, Hu Xiaosheng, and I saw this out of the corner of my eye. Actually, I have seen it many times over the years, just sitting up here, collecting dust. It never occurred to me that such a priceless treasure would be lying around forgotten."

"Because you still have much to learn," an old cracked voice said.

Jiayi turned and saw an elderly man hobbling toward them. As he approached them, he looked at her with very familiar eyes. He smiled and his eyes glistened. He knew who she was too.

"I'm starting to realize that," Zhihao said as he placed the seal on a nearby table. The three of them stood around it, each marveling in its magnificence.

"But you did find it," he said. "And that is what matters."

Jiayi tore her eyes from the seal and looked at the old man again. He smiled as if he too had seen her before. "So, you finally found me," he said.

"I didn't even know I was looking for you," she said. "Were you looking for me?"

"I've been waiting for you for...oh, well over seventy years now," he said.

"But...how? Why?" she asked.

"My sister once told me that she used to have these fantastical dreams," he said. "Dreams of another life. Dreams of a young woman at the court of an empress who had wild adventures."

"Your sister dreamed of me?" she asked.

"I wasn't sure for a long time. My sister thought her dreams were premonitions of herself reincarnated in a future life," he said.

"You think my dreams are of past lives?" she asked.

"I don't know," he said. "I need to know more. Have you inhabited the lives of people who have lived at the same time? Like you could be Lady Cai and another lady of Dagguang's court, depending on the items you were holding?"

"I can," Jiayi said.

"And have you ever been someone who is living now? Maybe someone who touched an item many years ago but is still alive?"

Jiayi thought about the woman who gave Zhihao his hatpin, the woman he called Rebecca. "I believe so," she said. "At least, I don't think the woman is dead. I suppose she could be..."

"She is alive," Zhihao quickly confirmed, knowing whom she was thinking of.

"And can you control the people you inhabit? Can you make them do certain things that they normally wouldn't?" he asked.

"I'm not sure," she said. "I usually just allow their

emotions, their movements to take me along. I don't feel in control. But sometimes I can hold them back, just for a moment. Like if I need someone to say something specific, I can keep my host from reacting, but it feels like holding back the tide. Eventually, the host will break free."

"Interesting..." Hu Xiaosheng mumbled.

"How do you know all this?" Jiayi asked.

The old man waved her question off. "Oh, I don't know anything. Only speculating. Special people has been something of an interest of mine. I'm always looking out for instances of women with unique abilities in my research. But the point is that you are not just a reincarnation of my sister. You are much more powerful than that."

"Powerful?" she asked.

"You are...hmm...like a tunnel. A tunnel linking the past and the present. Think of it as a channel between two large bodies of water. You thought you were just traveling one way, traveling into the past. But now you know that the knowledge and abilities of the people you touch, they can travel into our time."

"Yes!" she exclaimed. "Like the languages and my ability to fight. I brought those skills with me from the past into the present."

"Exactly!" he said. "I don't know exactly what you are, my dear, or why you have these abilities, but I do know you are extraordinary. I've never come across anyone like you. And your future is boundless."

Jiayi's eyes welled up with tears. She couldn't believe how the old man spoke to her with such kindness, such hope. She never imagined she could ever have any kind of future, and now her future was wide open. For the first time, she was daring to dream while she was awake.

Zhihao had not stopped staring at the seal. "You had it here the whole time," he said.

"Of course," Hu Xiaosheng said. "I had to keep it safe. No one ever checks in the library for such things. And this way, I could keep an eye on it."

"But you knew I was looking for it," Zhihao said. "Why didn't you just tell me where it was?"

"What good would that have done?" Hu Xiaosheng asked. "You wouldn't have *earned* the accolades the empress wants to lay upon you. And how would I have known if you were worthy?"

"Worthy of what?" Zhihao asked.

"Worthy of being my student," Hu Xiaosheng said.

"I thought I already was your student," Zhihao said.

Hu Xiaosheng waved him off. "You were too arrogant. Thought you already knew everything. And you wouldn't have learned to depend on this incredible girl. You would always have thought she was beneath you."

"That...that is probably true," Zhihao said, and Jiayi blushed. "So, what does it mean for me to be your student?"

"You are not going to be my student," Hu Xiaosheng said, enunciating every word.

"But you just said—" Zhihao started, but Hu Xiaosheng interrupted him.

"You will not be my only student. I will only take both of you as my students. You will work together or not at all," Hu Xiaosheng said, crossing his arms in a sense of finality.

"I'm ready to learn anything and everything," Jiayi said. "My mind feels...empty, like it is waiting to be filled."

"Well?" Hu Xiaosheng asked, looking at Zhihao.

"Well...sure. I mean, of course," Zhihao said with a crooked half-smile. "I think that Jiayi and I work well together. Why not keep a good thing going?"

"Excellent," Hu Xiaosheng said.

"But will the empress let me?" Jiayi asked. "After we give her the seal, she will certainly want me back at court."

"Just leave the empress to me," Hu Xiaosheng said with a wry smile.

TWENTY-ONE

*S*hortly after their meeting with Hu Xiaosheng, Zhihao sent a message to the empress letting her know they had found her item and had returned to Peking. The empress lost no time in responding. She sent a palace guard to fetch Jiayi and ordered Zhihao to present the item to her at a formal audience first thing in the morning. He was surprised she didn't send for him immediately, but he supposed it would be odd for him to show up so late in the day outside of a time when she usually held audiences. He barely even had a chance to say goodbye to Jiayi as she was whisked away in an enclosed sedan chair.

Zhihao returned to his office. He was glad to be back. If he and Jiayi had not found the seal, he might never have been back here again. He was pleased to see that all of his books, notes, and artifacts were just where he had left them. He paced the room for a bit. Straightened his stacks of papers. Then he straightened them again. Everything had worked out perfectly. They found the seal. Jiayi could return to the empress. He would be rewarded.

Why did he feel so unsettled?

He was straightening the papers on his desk for the third time when he heard a knock at the door.

"You made it back!" Lian said with a broad smile that looked even more dazzling in his bright white suit. "When you didn't send me a letter, I thought maybe you had fallen off the edge of the map."

"I very nearly did," Zhihao said, remembering the cave-in that nearly crushed the lot of them. "But good to know I would have been missed."

"Oh, I wouldn't go that far," Lian said. "We were all just debating how long you had to be gone before we started divvying up your things."

Zhihao smirked. He and Lian had been friends for a long time. They had schooled together in England, but Lian was much more interested in the political side of history than the digging part.

"Where are you off to?" Zhihao asked. "You look like you are going to a funeral."

Lian waved him off as he tugged at his cuffs. "I had a meeting. So, how did everything go?"

Zhihao nodded. "Fine. Everything went...just fine."

Lian cocked his head. "Are you sure about that? You... found whatever it was the empress sent you to find, then?"

"Oh, yes, I found it. We found it..."

"We?" Lian prodded. "Oh, come on. Are you going to tell me the story or am I going to drag it out of you bit by bit?"

"It's...complicated," Zhihao hedged. "But, there is a girl. She is...a sort of court historian, you might say. The empress sent her with me to find the artifact."

"A female court historian?" Lian asked. "That is incredible. Why has no one outside the court heard of her?"

"The empress keeps her rather close. She doesn't want anyone else to know about her."

"Poor dear," Lian replied. "She must feel rather trapped."

"Indeed," Zhihao said.

"And you...like this girl?" Lian asked.

"I...No, not like that. She is sweet and smart, but too... innocent, I suppose. But I feel the need to protect her. To help her."

"To protect her from whom?" Lian asked. "The empress?"

"Maybe," Zhihao said, running his fingers through his hair. "What if...what if you could...I can't even say the words. It is treason to even think what I am thinking."

"Treason?" Lian asked. "I like the sound of that. Now you must tell me."

Zhihao looked at Lian and considered him for a moment. Was he joking, only looking for some light entertainment? Or was he serious? Did he have revolutionary leanings? Were they more than leanings?

"You...umm...you have no love for the Qing, do you?" asked Zhihao.

"Ha! You should know me better than that. You know I fought the order to return to China for two years. They practically had to drag me back in chains."

That was true. Lian tried every avenue save marrying a British girl to get to stay in England when they finished their education. He loved his country and his parents too much to dare consider marrying a white woman. Yet he never missed an opportunity to complain about the Qing and the empress.

"If you could single-handedly bring down the Qing Empire, would you do it?" Zhihao asked.

"Without question," Lian said without missing a heartbeat.

"Even if it meant ruining the life of someone you care for?" Zhihao asked.

"You mean the court girl?" Lian asked. Zhihao nodded. Lian let out a long sigh. "Is there another way? Can you get the girl out first?"

"There is no time," Zhihao said. "She is already back at the palace. I have to return the artifact to the empress in the morning. Either I return it and forget about using it against the empress, or I keep and it and possibly start a revolution now. I don't even have time to get my family out of the city, much less the girl."

"Wait," Lian said. "The artifact the empress sent you to find could be used to dethrone her? What is it?"

Zhihao held his breath for a moment, deciding whether or not to trust his friend. He reached over and pulled a cloth sheet back, revealing the seal.

"Okay..." Lian said. "Is that what I think it is? Is that—"

"The emperor's seal," Zhihao confirmed.

"The emperor's seal!" Lian repeated. He slapped his hands together, spun around, put his hands on his head. He seemed unsure of how to react, so he was just flailing. "That...oh my God. That is the emperor's seal. Are you kidding me? Where was it? Why...why did the empress not have it herself?"

"That's exactly it," Zhihao said, not wanting to reveal where he found it. "This had been missing for over sixty years. The Qing have not had the Mandate of Heaven in three generations. Why are they still on the throne?"

"Because people are willing to hand over power if they think it is easier," Lian said. "People rarely act in their own self-interest."

"And you think keeping the seal will be in the best interest of all Chinese?" Zhihao asked.

"I think ridding China of the Qing plague is the best course of action, however it comes about," Lian said. "But you don't agree?"

"I don't know what to think," Zhihao said. "I don't like the Qing on the throne either. But who would be better? Some warlord? Some idealist who has no idea how to actually govern?"

"There would be a difficult era of transition, that is certain," Lian said. "When has setting up a new government ever been done without bloodshed? Even the empress has killed to keep her place secure."

"But whose blood would be shed in this case?" Zhihao said. "The Qing? Or those who stand against them? Me? My family?"

"All of the above?" Lian said.

"And the girl," Zhihao said. "I would have betrayed her. She thinks we are friends, a team. If I don't show up tomorrow, I can never see her again."

"Is that a price you are willing to pay?" Lian asked.

Zhihao didn't think so. He had already lost Rebecca. Could he lose Jiayi too? Once again would his own bad decisions cause a rift between him and a woman he cared about that could never be healed? Would the empress hold Jiayi responsible? Would he be able to ever forgive himself if the empress put her to death because he stole the seal?

"Are you involved in this kind of stuff?" Zhihao asked. "Would you know who I could give the seal to?"

"I...know some people," Lian said. "But would the revolution start right now? No. These things take time, planning. We need to gather support, momentum. You should have told me what you were looking for, then I could have been ready when you returned. But now...I don't know. If you don't show up tomorrow, the empress will know what you did and that you plan to use it against her. She probably already has a plan in place just in case she does not get the seal back."

"So...you think I should just give it to her like I promised?" Zhihao asked.

"Only you can answer that, friend," Lian said. "But know that this is not the only chance we will have to overthrow the Qing. Their days are numbered. Will it happen sooner if you keep the seal? Maybe. But don't make the mistake of thinking that the destiny of an entire country rests with you.

"A country is made up of her people, not one man. The people's rule, the people's power, the people's livelihood. These are the basis of a good government."

And just like that, Zhihao knew where Lian stood. The teachings of Dr. Sun were unmistakable.

"You don't just know people involved in the rebel groups, do you?" Zhihao said. "You are one of them."

"I won't deny it," Lian said. "But we must all be cautious."

"Why have you never told me before?" Zhihao said.

"You never really seemed interested in changing the status quo," Lian said. "Though, I considered it when we first returned from England. I thought maybe your broken heart would be ripe for planting new ideas."

"Then, why didn't you?" Zhihao asked.

"I was young and still new to the movement myself. I was unsure of how to recruit new members safely. By the time I started growing my confidence and getting more involved, you seemed to have resettled in your life here. I didn't think it was my place to disturb you. But it sounds like you have been having doubts since before this seal fell into your lap."

"What man can call himself a Han and not have

doubts?" Zhihao nearly spat. "I think many of our coun-
trymen have settled for life the way it is under the Qing, but
they would not think twice about raising their fists against
them when given the chance."

"The Qing would agree with you," Lian said. "They are
terrified the Han will rise up against them. We outnumber
them ten to one. Why would we not?"

"Why haven't we, then?" Zhihao asked.

"Fear of the unknown. Fear of the risks, of self-sacrifice.
Many reasons. But it's only a matter of time before the dam
breaks."

"So, what should I do? You aren't helping me make a
decision," Zhihao said.

"I can't answer that for you," Lian said. "But whatever
you decide, you can't go back to the way things were before.
You can't deny the revolutionary blood coursing through
your veins." Lian gripped Zhihao's arms and stared deep
into his eyes. "You know what is coming. You know what is
happening. You might not be able to start the revolution
today, but you can't stop it from coming. Join me, brother."

Zhihao was mesmerized by Lian's words, by his passion.
Zhihao had felt his disdain for the Manchu ruling class
growing for a long time, and meeting the empress had done
nothing to stem that trend. If anything, she made him hate
the Manchu more. The empress was ruling without
authority and wielded her power with cruelty. When he
thought about the way she held Jiayi captive, his fists
instinctively clenched.

Jiayi.

He couldn't just leave her there, no matter how much he
wanted to stop the empress. If anything, he had to help
overthrow the Manchu rulers for her. To help free her, even
though she was one of them. But she was not of the ruling

class. She was Manchu, but she was just as oppressed as any Han. When he thought about Jiayi, he felt a fire in his belly. Without her, he didn't think he could find the strength needed to be part of the revolution.

He would return the seal, but only to save Jiayi and overthrow the Manchu once and for all.

TWENTY-TWO

$\mathcal{T}$he sedan chair seemed to arrive only moments after Zhihao sent the message to the empress letting her know that they had found the seal. As the chair-bearer lifted the flap to the chair, Jiayi hesitated before stepping in and felt her heart sink. She was getting back into her cage. Even though she, Zhihao, and Hu Xiaosheng had agreed it was for the best, she was afraid that if she willingly went back to the empress, she would never have another chance to get away. Standing at the foot of the stairs to the library, she looked left and right, wondering if she had any chance of getting away if she fled. She thought that the chair-bearers might not chase her if she did. They were not guards, after all. She looked back at Zhihao, and he gave her a reassuring smile.

"I will see you in a few short hours," he said.

She nodded and climbed into the chair.

"Princess Der Ling!" she gasped when she realized she was not alone in the chair. Her instinct was to kneel before the princess, but it was not possible in the chair. She bent at the waist instead and kept her eyes to the floor.

"Sit up," Der Ling said.

Jiayi did as she was ordered but kept her head bent down.

"So, you found the thing?" Der Ling asked. "You really found the emperor's seal?"

"I...We did, your highness," Jiayi said. "Zhihao and I were successful in our mission."

Der Ling was silent for a moment, then she started to laugh. Jiayi lifted her eyes for a moment. The princess was shaking her head as she laughed, as if in disbelief.

"I can't believe it," the princess finally said. "All this time I have wondered if you could really be true. If you were just making up such fantastical stories. Even though the empress has believed in your abilities for years, I thought she must be crazy. That you must be far more clever than you let on to be able to fool the empress."

Jiayi felt the corner of her mouth lift. At least the princess was giving Jiayi enough credit to think her clever; that was more respect than most people gave her. But she had no idea how to respond. Should she thank her? Tell her she was wrong? The safest option was always to stay quiet, so that was what she did.

"Look at me, Jiayi," the princess said after a moment.

Jiayi lifted her head, but kept her eyes downcast. Der Ling reached over and just touched the tip of Jiayi's chin with her finger, urging her to look up with barely a movement.

"I said, look at me," she whispered.

Jiayi did as she was ordered.

Der Ling was not a princess by blood. She was actually a foreigner. Her mother was French and her father was the Chinese foreign minister to France. She had been born and raised in France, but the family had returned to China only a couple of years before due to the minister's failing health. When the family appeared before the empress upon their return, the empress had become smitten with the charming Der Ling and asked that she join her household as a lady-in-waiting, to which Der Ling readily agreed. She quickly became the empress's favorite, and as a gift, the empress styled Der Ling as "princess," a title Der Ling was more than happy to accept and exploit to the fullest.

Der Ling's bright shining eyes were mesmerizing to Jiayi. They were unlike any eyes Jiayi had seen before, and her face was white, her nose pronounced. She had thin, painted eyebrows and outlined her eyes with kohl. She wore the largest, most ornate *batou*, and jewels danged from holes in her earlobes that Jiayi thought must have been excruciatingly painful.

Finally, after what seemed like minutes, Der Ling removed her fingertip from Jiayi's chin and nodded. "There is nothing but sincerity in you, is there?" she finally asked, but didn't seem to want an answer. "You look terrified. Are you afraid of me?"

"I...I don't know why you are here," Jiayi said, which surprised her. Even the most bold of court minister was often cowed by the mere presence of the Princess Der Ling. Jiayi was shocked she could make a croak, much less a coherent sentence.

"I want you to do something for me," Der Ling said. Out of her sleeve, she pulled a sheathed dagger. Jiayi gasped and recoiled. "Calm down, girl," Der Ling said with a roll of her eyes. "I want you to touch this for me. Tell me who it belonged to."

The dagger was curved and ornately carved. The hilt was shaped like a phoenix and the whole thing was encrusted with jewels. It looked more ceremonial than functional, but Jiayi knew that even blunt knives could draw blood.

"Does...does the empress know?" Jiayi asked. "She doesn't like for me to use my powers without her orders."

"She doesn't know where you are," the princess said.

"But...the summons..." Jiayi said, confused.

"I intercepted the message from Zhihao," the princess admitted. "I just bribed the eunuch who was delivering the note. I told you to return. I wanted to speak with you first. Learn for myself if your powers truly were real."

"Where...where are we going?" Jiayi asked as she scooted as closely to the door as she could. The flaps to the chair were tied tightly. She wasn't sure she could escape very quickly if she needed to...unless she used the dagger to cut the ties loose.

"We are headed to the Forbidden City," Der Ling said. "It is late. You will slip to your room unnoticed. In the morning, I will tell the empress you have only just returned and she will be none the wiser. She will be so excited to get her grubby little hands on the seal, she won't think to ask why you did not return sooner."

Jiayi felt her jaw drop at the disrespectful way Der Ling spoke of the empress, but Der Ling just waved her hand as though it was of no consequence.

"She is not feeling well anyway," she continued. "She has not left her porcelain bowl for hours."

Jiayi shook her head in shock. Did this spoiled foreigner have no respect for the elderly?

"Forget about her," Der Ling said, holding the dagger out. "Touch this. Tell me who the owner was."

Jiayi's hands were clasped in her lap. She often held them together to keep from touching anything by accident. She wrung them together now. She didn't know what was going on, but she did not want to make an enemy of Der Ling. She finally nodded and held her hands palms up. Der Ling smiled and dropped the dagger into her hands.

Jiayi was weeping. She couldn't help it. Something terrible had happened. Something that shook her to the core, but she had no idea what. She raised her head and wiped her eyes so she could see. She was in a room she had not been in before, but it was exquisitely furnished. She looked down at her dress and recognized her style of clothes. She was in the Tang Dynasty. But she certainly was not Lady Meirong.

"The emperor approaches!" a voice rang out.

The emperor! She stood and tried to calm her host and then kneeled as the door opened.

"My dear," the man said as he rushed to her side and lifted her to her feet. He embraced her tightly, and she hugged him back gently, surprised at such affection from him. "How are you?" he asked as he pulled back and gently cupped her face. "Are you injured?"

Jiayi's eyes widened in surprise and then touched her chest and stomach, checking for injuries. "I...I don't think so."

The emperor sighed in relief. "That is good. Do not worry, the bitch will pay for what she did."

"I...certainly hope so," Jiayi said, even though she had no idea what was going on. She needed to find out quickly so she could tell Der Ling. And where was the dagger?

"She thinks that just because she is the empress, I cannot punish her," the emperor said. "But she will learn that she cannot control me any longer. I should just depose her, put her to death, and name you my empress." He was angry now, stomping around the room. To Jiayi, this seemed vaguely familiar.

"You mean...Empress...Wang?" Jiayi asked hopefully.

"Who else would I be talking about, you silly thing?" the emperor asked.

"Forgive me," Jiayi said, trying to act sad and scared while controlling her excitement. She knew who she was. Empress Wang was the proper first wife of Emperor Gaozong. Which meant Jiayi was the woman who would become Empress Wu.

"I...I am still so upset," Jiayi said as she slumped down into a chair. "I'm not thinking straight."

Gaozong ran to her and kneeled in front of her. He kneeled! The stories were right. Gaozong was so enamored with the young Wu Mei that he humbled himself before her.

"I know, my love," he said. "That is why I have brought you a gift." He reached into his robe and pulled out the dagger that Der Ling had given her. She reached out and ran her fingers over it. "If the empress ever sends an assassin after you again, I never want you to feel weak or powerless. You will always be protected."

"Thank you," Jiayi said as she took the dagger from him. She held it up and watched as the jewels reflected the light from the room's braziers.

Jiayi gasped as she opened her eyes. She coughed as she tried to take a full breath. Der Ling was now sitting by her side instead of across from her, and she was patting her on the back.

"Thank the gods," Der Ling said in relief. "I was beginning to think you weren't coming back."

"Forgive me," Jiayi said. "It took a while for me to figure out who I was."

"But you did it?" Der Ling asked, her eyes sparkling. "You saw who the owner was? Tell me!"

"It was Empress Wu," Jiayi said confidently, and the two women smiled at each other.

"Yes!" Der Ling pumped her fist in the air in triumph and kicked her feet. She then hugged Jiayi and took the dagger from her. She kissed the dagger and held it in her arms like a precious baby. "I knew it. I knew you were the one."

"The empress will be ecstatic when she finds out," Jiayi said. But when Der Ling shot her a dark look, she wished she hadn't.

"The empress can never know about this," Der Ling said.

"But...the empress has been looking for Empress Wu," Jiayi said, confused.

"And she can keep looking," Der Ling said as she moved back across from Jiayi. "This is my link. This dagger, I was sure it belonged to Empress Wu, but I had to know for certain. What did you see in your vision? What happened?"

"Not much," Jiayi said. "Gaozong gave it to her after Empress Wang tried to have her killed."

Der Ling nodded. "She carried this dagger with her for the rest of her life. We will need to get more visions of it. I believe this is no ordinary dagger."

"What do you mean?" Jiayi asked. "Not ordinary?"

"You'll see," Der Ling said. "As long as you keep having visions for me."

"But the empress won't like that—" Jiayi started to say.

"The empress must never know," Der Ling said. "Not yet, anyway. This will be our little secret."

"But..." Jiayi sighed and hemmed and hawed over her words. She couldn't say no to a princess, but if the empress found out, she would be furious. She could toss Jiayi out without a second thought, or worse. "I work for the empress. She gives me things to see. If I spend my energy on the dagger for you, I could become useless to her."

"I will make it worth your while," Der Ling said. She leaned forward on her knees and looked at Jiayi slyly. "What is it you want, Jiayi?"

To escape, Jiayi wanted to say but bit her tongue. She had no idea how much she could trust Der Ling, if at all. In the two years that Der Ling had been a lady-in-waiting, the two had barely exchanged more than passing pleasantries. Yet now, she was asking Jiayi to trust her with her life? After the changes and excitement of the last few days, this was the last thing she expected to happen.

But could this be another opportunity? She was working with Zhihao and would be taught by Hu Xiaosheng. Was this just another way for her to help herself and possibly gain another ally. If she could find a way to trust Der Ling, she could be a powerful friend. Der Ling was wealthy, well-educated, and knew people all over the world. Jiayi felt a tinge of greed in her chest. She wanted Der Ling's help, but if Der Ling betrayed her, it could cost her her life. She needed something in exchange.

"Are you loyal to the empress, princess?" Jiayi asked.

"Of course I am," Der Ling said without an ounce of sincerity. "I am loyal to the end of my days. Aren't you?"

Jiayi nodded. "To the end of my days."

Der Ling sat back and smiled. "Oh, Jiayi. I think this is the start of a beautiful friendship."

TWENTY-THREE

The next morning, bright and early, Zhihao returned to the Forbidden City, accompanied by Hu Xiaosheng. They were immediately shown into the empress's audience hall. As the empress arrived, Jiayi was also brought in. She, Zhihao, and Hu Xiaosheng all kowtowed.

"Rise," the empress said as soon as she was seated. The three of them sat up, but remained on their knees, as was proper. The empress looked harried; her hair was off-center, her robe wrinkled, and her makeup unfinished. She had undoubtedly prepared herself in a hurry, anxious to get her seal. "Well?" she asked.

"Your Majesty," Zhihao said, "I am pleased to inform you that the mission was a success and we have found the emperor's seal."

The empress held her hand out. "Give it to me," she said.

Zhihao reached into his bag and carefully pulled out the seal. The whole room gasped and the empress cried out.

"You did it!" she gasped. "You have greatly pleased us."

The empress's head eunuch took the seal from Zhihao and handed it gently to the empress.

"It looks just how I imagined," she said as tears fell down her face. "Gather the ministers and my worthless nephew. We must meet today, this very afternoon!"

The eunuch bowed and left to make the arrangements. The empress held onto the seal, stroking it as if it were one of her little dogs.

"You have done a great deed for me, Zhihao," the empress said. "How can I ever repay you?"

"Your Majesty honors me," Zhihao said. "I would never have found it without the aid of Lady Jiayi."

"Oh, of course, of course," the empress said. "Isn't she a treasure? I have missed her so. I am glad she has been returned to court."

Zhihao glanced at Jiayi and saw her biting her lower lip. But they knew the empress would expect Jiayi to return.

"I must also introduce you to Hu Xiaosheng," Zhihao said. "He was the brother of Lady Cai, and it was he who kept the seal safe all these years."

Hu Xiaosheng bowed.

"I cannot wait to hear the whole story of how the seal was found," the empress said. "But if this is true, I am also in your debt, Hu Xiaosheng."

"I would never hold a debt against the throne, Your Majesty," Hu Xiaosheng said. "All I have done has been for the good of the empire."

"Indeed," the empress said. "Well, whatever you need, you must only ask it of us."

"I believe Your Majesty is aware of the archeological missions the foreigners are conducting on our soil?" Hu Xiaosheng asked.

"Indeed, we are," the empress replied curtly.

"It is my only wish, and I believe the wish of all Chinese, that these priceless heirlooms remain here in China," Hu Xiaosheng said.

"We are in agreement," the empress said.

"It is my understanding that you promised young Zhihao a museum if he succeeded in finding the seal," Hu Xiaosheng pressed.

The empress licked her lips and proceeded to speak slowly. "We did this thing, but considering how the seal was procured," she said, looking at Jiayi, "explaining such an endowment would be difficult."

Zhihao nodded slightly. So, the empress was not planning on keeping her word. He should have known as much. It only reaffirmed his desire to speak more with Lian about China's future. At least Hu Xiaosheng was prepared for this outcome.

"I could not agree more, Your Majesty," Hu Xiaosheng said. "Instead, I would beg of you to allow Zhihao and Jiayi to continue searching for China's artifacts on their own. They can collect them, and I can keep them safe in the university library. After we have a large store of items, then we can approach the council with a request for a museum. After all, there is no point in having a museum if we have nothing to put in it. Let us procure the items first, then we will build the museum later."

"I am in favor of this plan," the empress demurred. "Yet you wish to take Jiayi with you? Are you aware that she is precious to me?"

"I am aware, Your Majesty," Hu Xiaosheng said. "Your plan of sending her with Zhihao to locate the seal worked almost too well, did it not, Zhihao?"

"It did, sir, Your Majesty," Zhihao said. "I could not have located the seal without her help."

"If you allow her to work with Zhihao, supervised by myself, as a senior historian but one too old to go out into the field, Jiayi could be not only precious to you, but useful," Hu Xiaosheng explained. "Think of what she could accomplish for all of China—in *your* name. Now that you have found the seal, you have secured the throne for your nephew. Next, you could preserve China's history for generations to come!"

The empress mulled this over for several moments. Zhihao was certain that Jiayi had stopped breathing while she waited for the empress's answer.

It was clear to Zhihao that Hu Xiaosheng knew what he was doing. He was playing on the empress's weaknesses and vanity. Everyone knew that the Manchu only held a tenuous grasp on the throne. With the emperor's seal, her grip on it was a little more firm, but how much stock the ministers, the nobles, and the rest of the country would put into it as a symbol of their right to rule was still unclear. Yet he was giving the empress credit for finding it...and the responsibility to do more. By preserving China's history, the empress was blurring the line that separated the Han and Manchu, creating one China. Perhaps this was why she had also signed the edict allowing Han and Manchu people to marry. She wanted to effectively breed their differences out.

"Very well," the empress finally said. "Jiayi will continue to be a member of my court. And when you are not looking for something specific, she will remain here with me. But when her services as needed, I will allow her to assist Zhihao as he searches for relics. But she must be carefully guarded. Where is Eunuch Lo?"

"I'm very sorry, Your Majesty," Jiayi said softly. "But Eunuch Lo is dead. He died protecting me."

"What?" the empress shrieked. "When? How? This is unacceptable. Who was guarding her honor?"

"It was...umm...only toward the end of the journey," Zhihao stammered. "And then Hu Xiaosheng...he joined us...and..."

"I am sure we can trust that Zhihao Shaoye returned Jiayi to us as she left," a strange looking woman to the empress's right said.

"I don't like this," the empress muttered. "I don't like it at all. What am I to do now, Der Ling?"

Zhihao nodded to himself. Princess Der Ling. He had heard of her before. The foreign daughter of a Chinese minister. That explained her odd appearance.

"We can appoint a new guardian for her," Der Ling said. "I know someone who would be perfect."

The empress sighed. "Fine, fine. You deal with it, my dear. I have too many other things to worry about."

Der Ling bowed. "Of course, your majesty." As she rose, Zhihao thought he saw her give a small smile to Jiayi, but Jiayi kept her face still. He remembered that Jiayi had said she had no friends among the court ladies. He would have to ask her about Der Ling later.

"Of course, Jiayi will not be able to leave the palace until we find a new guardian for her," the empress said.

"Of course, Your Majesty," they all said with a bow.

"If there is nothing else?" she asked, standing.

"No, Your Majesty," they all said as they kowtowed.

"Good. I must prepare to meet with the ministers." The empress and all of her attendants then left the room. Zhihao, Jiayi, and Hu Xiaosheng all took a deep breath of relief as they stood.

"So, everything worked out as we had hoped," Zhihao said.

"Hope," Hu Xiaosheng said, tapping his nose, "but be cautious."

"Couldn't the same be said of any situation?" Zhihao asked.

"Humph," Hu Xiaosheng scoffed. "Such a pessimist. You will learn, my boy...you will learn." With that, he turned and walked out of the audience hall.

"I cannot wait to spend more time with him," Jiayi said when they were alone. "He knows so much. Not just about history, but about me. If anyone can help me make sense of this, it will be him."

"Will you walk me out?" Zhihao asked. Jiayi nodded and turned toward the door. "It looks as though we will be working together for the foreseeable future," Zhihao said as they walked in the sunshine.

"Everything did seem to work out rather sweetly," Jiayi replied. "We found the seal, the empress is happy, Hu Xiaosheng is going to be a teacher to me..."

"As will I," Zhihao said. "If you are still interested."

"We are *both* supposed to be students," she said.

"I can be both a student and a teacher," he said.

"What can you teach me that Hu Xiaosheng cannot?" she asked.

"Well, English, for one. You said you wanted to learn," he said. Jiayi bit her lip and turned away from him. Zhihao followed her. "What is wrong?" he asked. "What did I say?"

"That night in the inn," Jiayi said. "You were quite cruel."

"I know," Zhihao said, lightly grabbing her elbow and turning her to him. She did not look up, but kept her eyes to the ground. "And I apologized. I was terrible to you, and I am sorry. Is that not enough?"

"I don't know," Jiayi said. "I don't know you. I do not

know if you are sincere or are simply a very good liar. Or someone who knows how to trick women. Or someone who is out for his own gains."

He felt pained at that. Not because she was wrong, but because she was right, at least partly. He did want to help her and preserve China's history. But he also wanted the glory that could go along with being China's preeminent archeologist. He also wanted to stay close to the throne so he could play a central role in overthrowing the Manchu. He could not tell Jiayi that, though. Even though she wished to escape the empress, he did not think she would support a coup against the Manchu. After all, she was Manchu as well. He would have to get to know her better before he learned her thoughts on that matter.

"The same could be said of anyone," Zhihao said, deflecting. "I don't know you. I don't know what you hope to gain out of this relationship, out of this new assignment from the empress. You kept things from me too. I thought you were a lady, and then I find that you cannot even read…"

Jiayi held up her hand. "Stop talking, please. Of course I have kept things from you. I still have my secrets. And you are allowed to have yours. But I would never deceive you. I would never hurt you. I would never risk or threaten your life. You at least know me that well, wouldn't you agree?"

Zhihao breathed out of his nose. "Yes, I would agree. But you could not say the same of me? Is that what you are saying?"

"I would like to trust you," she said, and Zhihao met her gaze. He looked deep, as though he was looking for something. There was something inside her he wanted, that he needed. He felt as though there was an answer hidden in her eyes, but he didn't know what the question was. But did he want Jiayi? Was he looking for Rebecca in her eyes? Hu Xiaosheng did say that the river of time flowed both ways. Did Rebecca see through Jiayi's eyes as Jiayi did through hers? Could Zhihao see them both staring back at him?

Jiayi blinked, breaking the spell, and turned to walk again. "I would like to," she repeated. "But such trust takes time. I am anxious to work with you and learn from you, but when it comes to trust, please do not rush me. I have lived a lonely life. I have no friends, no family. I do not know what it means to trust, to befriend. I must ask for your patience."

"As long as we can work together while we are building that trust, then, yes, I will wait for you," Zhihao said.

"Good," Jiayi said with a sharp nod and a broad smile.

TWENTY-FOUR

"So, what happens now?" Jiayi asked. "The empress wants us to find China's lost relics. Where will we begin?"

"Honestly, we could begin almost anywhere," Zhihao said. "As long as humans have existed, there have been civilizations here in China. You can't throw a stone in this country without hitting something with historical importance."

"But you know that isn't what the empress wants," Jiayi said. "She doesn't want just any old thing found. We have to find amazing things! Fascinating things! Things that when people enter your museum, they will take your breath away."

Zhihao chuckled. "I've said before that you should be a writer. You have quite a way with words."

"As soon as I learn to read and write, I will," she said.

"I will talk to Hu Xiaosheng, consult my books. I'll see what the foreign archeologists are looking for. Then we can come up with a list of things we should focus on," Zhihao explained.

"I cannot wait to learn more about history," Jiayi said. "Can you tell me more about Prince Junjie?"

Zhihao tossed his head back and laughed out loud. "Can't stop thinking about that handsome man, can you?"

"It's not just that," she said, trying to act nonchalant. "I would love to know more about the people I have met, the people I have been. Lady Cai, for example! You said she was disgraced. What did you mean by that? What about Empress Wu? One of her relics would certainly thrill the empress."

"Slow down!" Zhihao said. "I can't teach you everything in one day. But Prince Junjie is easy. We don't know much, but he died quite young."

Jiayi stopped and felt her heart freeze. She tried to keep her face impassive, but was not sure she was doing a very good job.

"What do you mean?" she asked. "In battle?"

"Oh, no, nothing like that," Zhihao said. "Treachery of some sort. Someone murdered him, we think. We don't really know all the details."

"I don't like the sound of that," Jiayi said, her heart racing. All of a sudden, she wanted to fly to him, make sure he was all right.

"You could help rewrite history," Zhihao said.

"What did you say?" Jiayi asked, and it was as though a light went off in her mind.

"You could find out the truth," Zhihao said. "You could find out what really happened and could change or clarify what we currently know about past people and events."

Jiayi knew what he meant—revising history books to reflect the truth. But what if she could do more than that? What if she could actually rewrite history? She didn't know if she could influence the people she possessed. She had always thought she was just water in a vessel, flowing the way her host went, saying and doing what her host had already done. She was merely an observer. But what if she was wrong? What if she could force her host to do as she willed? What if she could change history? She thought about the time she was Rebecca, how Rebecca wanted to cry and beg Zhihao not to leave her. She had stopped her, held the tears back, at least for a moment. Could she exert more control?

What if she could save Prince Junjie's life?

"Jiayi?" Zhihao said, snapping his fingers in front of her face. "Jiayi, are you there?"

"What?" she asked, looking at him.

"For a moment I thought you had touched something and were lost in the past," he said. "What were you in such deep thought about?"

"What if you are right?" she asked. "What if I can change the past?"

THANK YOU FOR READING!

Jiayi and Zhihao will return in *The Empress's Dagger*, available now!
Subscribe to my mailing list so you will never miss a new release!
http://amandarobertswrites.com/subscribe-touching-time/

ABOUT THE AUTHOR

 Amanda Roberts is a USA Today best-selling author who has been living in China since 2010. She has an MA in English from the University of Central Missouri and has been published in magazines, newspapers, and anthologies around the world. Amanda can be found all over the Internet, but her home is AmandaRobertsWrites.com.

facebook.com/AmandaRobertsWrites

instagram.com/amandarobertswrites

bookbub.com/authors/amanda-roberts-2bfe99dd-ea16-4614-a696-84116326dcd1

goodreads.com/Amanda_Roberts

ABOUT THE PUBLISHER

VISIT OUR WEBSITE
TO SEE ALL OF OUR HIGH QUALITY BOOKS:

http://www.redempresspublishing.com

Quality trade paperbacks, downloads, audio books, and books
in foreign languages in genres such as historical, romance,
mystery, and fantasy.